Jenni savors her time with the Lord and His creation.

She found an area of beach in the park reserve and walked to the water's edge to watch the sun spread its colors over the water. Trey was probably standing on this same beach, watching this same sunrise, just a few miles up the shoreline. She would like to be watching it with him. She would like to spend a lifetime watching sunrises with him, but she wanted something else even more. She turned on the tape player and slipped off her shoes. The morning sand felt cool against her bare feet.

As the music began, Jenni lifted her arms toward heaven and moved slowly and gracefully. Sounds of stringed instruments and the background of the ocean surf wafted through the air. There were no words on the instrumental, but Jenni knew the lyrics by heart. She sang Psalm 42 silently as she danced. "As the deer pants for streams of water, so my soul pants for you, O God."

This was Jenni's worship. Like David in the Psalms, she danced before the Lord in her joy of His love. It provided the surrender she needed to open herself completely to His will.

LOUISE TUCKER JONES is a native of Oklahoma where she lives with her husband Carl. They are the parents of four, one who was the special inspiration for the children in this story. Louise speaks often to women's groups and at other conferences. Though this is her first fiction publication, she co-authored *Extraordinary Kids: Nurturing and Championing Your Child with Special Needs* (Focus on the Family). The book was a Gold Medallion Book Award winner. She has also written for several magazines.

Dance from the Heart

Louise Tucker Jones

Heartsong Presents

For Carl, who fills my heart with love and my life with adventure.

Thanks to Anne Blasdel for sharing her expertise on ballet and the theater, and a special thanks to my HHBC Prayer Pals: Pam, Mary Lou, Glenda, Marqueeta, Jimmie, Sheri, Barbara, Cindy, Debra, and Dotti.

A note from the author:

I love to hear from my readers! You may correspond with me by writing:

Louise Tucker Jones
Author Relations
PO Box 719
Uhrichsville, OH 44683

ISBN 1-57748-965-9

DANCE FROM THE HEART

Cover design by Robyn Martins.

PRINTED IN THE U.S.A.

one

Jenni Lawson shifted uncomfortably in the lightly padded chair, flipping her boarding pass back and forth between her fingers. She glanced at her watch. Still thirty minutes before her flight, and she had already been waiting nearly twice that long. But it was she, not Doug, who had insisted on leaving early, fearing a traffic jam, flat tire, or something crazy like having to go back home because she forgot her luggage.

Surveying the waiting travelers, she wondered if there were a single person besides herself who had never been on a plane. How in the world do you get to be twenty-four years old and never have flown on a plane? Most people didn't even believe her when she told them.

Jenni glanced at Doug, who sat sullenly beside her in the row of connecting chairs. She broke the thick silence that surrounded them. "You really don't have to wait for me to board."

"I want to wait. I thought I made that clear," Doug said sharply. "I also want to know why you're doing this."

"Doing what?" Jenni looked at him in surprise.

"Following some wild notion that takes you halfway across the country."

"Doug, we've been through this over and over." Jenni closed her eyes and rubbed her forehead with the tips of her fingers, praying she could keep from getting angry as she made yet one more explanation to Doug. "I have a job at a theater in Cocoa Beach. You know that!" She threw her hands up in frustration.

Doug got to his feet, paced a few steps, and then returned to his seat and spoke quietly to Jenni as if he were telling her a secret. "I also know that you've been offered a contract with a dance company right *here* in Oklahoma City," he said. Jenni didn't respond. Doug turned in his chair and leaned toward her, his voice escalating. "Do you have any idea how far Florida is from Oklahoma?"

"No, but I'm sure *you* do." She sighed and stared out the window with somber brown eyes, wondering why she had allowed him to bring her to the airport. She brushed invisible lint from her pale pink linen jacket and pants then toyed with the small cross pendant that accented her white silk blouse.

"It just so happens that I do know. I can't give you an exact figure because the mileage would vary according to the route one takes, but it is approximately 1300 miles. . . ."

Jenni pushed back her thick, dark, shoulder-length hair and crossed her slender legs. *I wish he would leave*, she thought to herself. How had they dated for so long with such differences? Doug, the efficient, predictable engineer, and she, the spontaneous, artistic sort. At first their differences had seemed to balance their relationship, but lately nothing seemed balanced in her life. She needed a change. Suddenly she realized that Doug was still railing at her side.

"Why don't you just admit you made an impulsive decision, Jenni?"

"Okay! Yes! I made an impulsive decision!" Jenni nearly screamed at him. Several people turned to look at them. Jenni took a deep breath and lowered her voice. "Doug, I realize that you have probably never done a spontaneous thing in your life. But I suddenly realized that I am twenty-four years old and have never even been on my own and decided to do something about it."

"So you decide to spend the summer in Florida with a scatter-brained friend."

Jenni jerked to her feet. "That's it! I've had it!" She began gathering her things. "I refuse to listen to you rant and rave a minute longer."

"I think 'rant and rave' is a poor choice of words," Doug said calmly.

Jenni's eyes danced with fire. "I'll use any words I choose, and speaking of choices, I want you to leave. Thanks for the ride, but we have nothing more to discuss."

"I'm sorry, Jenni." Doug was standing beside her. "I know Myra is your friend. It's just that she's so. . .unreliable and. . ."

Jenni closed her eyes and bit the inside of her lower lip, trying to control her anger. "It's almost time for my plane," she said wearily.

"And you're probably scared to death."

Jenni's hands trembled, more from anger than fear. The intercom cut off her intended curt reply. "Flight 225 to Orlando now boarding at Gate 10."

She threw her carry-on bag over her shoulder and grabbed her purse.

Doug took hold of her arm. "What about us, Jenni? Doesn't our future mean anything to you?"

"I'm not sure we have a future together, Doug." She saw the pain in his dark eyes and was sorry they were parting this way. She was fond of Doug, at least she had been. He shared her faith in God and seemed to understand her devotion to ballet. But when she told him about her plans to work in Florida for the summer, everything changed. Now she didn't see how she could possibly share her life with him. "I've got to go," Jenni said, trying to smile.

Doug kissed her lightly on the lips. "You'll be back before the summer is over. I know you will be."

She only shook her head as she walked away and meshed into the crowd of people.

"Jenni!" She looked back at Doug. "I love you! I know you'll be back."

The crowd moved Jenni forward. She handed the attendant her boarding pass and walked through the jetway and onto the plane. Icy fingers of fear gripped her and she wondered if Doug could possibly be right. Was she really ready for this?

Surprised at the enormity of the plane, Jenni searched for the seat numbers below the luggage rack. Finding her assigned seat, she settled herself in and looked out the window. She was leaving everything familiar to her for a job in a place she had never been, a place where she knew only one person, Myra. A slight shudder went through her. *Doug was right. I am scared. A part of me wants to stay and accept the security that a job with a local dance company offers. And what if I get to Florida and actually miss Doug and want to return? Or worse, what if I find I don't love him at all but still have to return at the end of the summer?*

As people filed down the aisle of the plane, Jenni tried to put all the negative thoughts out of her mind. A woman and a boy about ten years of age sat down in front of her. "Are you going to look out the window, Mom? Dad said you wouldn't." The child played with the shade on the window, and Jenni didn't hear the woman's reply.

Taking a couple of deep breaths, she leaned back in her seat and tried to relax. The last few weeks had been an emotional roller coaster. Her mother had burst into tears each time she mentioned Cocoa Beach. "If only I weren't an only child," she muttered to herself.

But the worst blow of all was the sudden death of her grandfather. As a child she had spent many summers in the hills of Tahlequah with her grandparents. She and her grandfather used to canoe down the river and hike the wooded trails. Jenni's father had died when she was four years old, and she suspected that her grandfather tried to do for her what her father would have done.

Her thoughts were suddenly interrupted by someone bumping her on the head with a bag while putting it in the overhead storage. She reached up to brush her dark hair away from her face and discovered that the gold comb was missing from her hair.

"I'm terribly sorry," a male voice addressed her. Jenni knew before she looked up that the man would be smiling. She could hear it in his voice. She tilted her head to see who had bumped her and looked into the bluest eyes she had ever seen. And just as she expected, he had a big smile on his lean, tanned face. From where she sat, he appeared to bc well over six feet tall. He ran his fingers through his blond hair as he looked at her quizzically. Suddenly Jenni realized she was staring and he was asking her a question for the second time.

"Are you hurt? I'm sorry about hitting you with my bag." The man settled himself into the aisle seat beside her, then looked in her direction.

"Oh, I'm fine. I just lost my comb," she said, putting her hand to the loose hair falling toward her face. She looked around on the floor, and the man lowered his head to help. His long, muscular arm reached over near Jenni's foot and retrieved the small gold comb.

"Is this it?" he asked, turning it over in his large hand.

"Yes, thank you." Jenni took the comb and placed it in her hair. She glanced toward her seatmate, again noticing his size. His long legs appeared cramped with the limited space between the seats. He was wearing spotless white slacks and a casual blue knit shirt that showed off his broad chest and matched the blue of his eyes perfectly. He turned his attention toward Jenni.

"Looks perfect," he said.

"Excuse me?"

"The comb," he said, pointing toward her hair. "It looks perfect."

Jenni felt her cheeks warm and wondered what was wrong with her. It wasn't as if men never paid her compliments, and this wasn't exactly what she would call a compliment.

"Thank you," she said and quickly turned her attention to the front of the plane where a steward, about her age, was directing their attention to emergency exits and procedures. She was surprised to see a young man instead of a woman.

Jenni listened and watched intently, but when he demonstrated the use of the oxygen mask, she felt a little panic and glanced around to see what other people were doing. Most were busy getting out books, positioning bags under the seats, and paying little attention to anyone else.

She looked back to the front, and the young man smiled warmly at her. Something in his expression told her he knew this was her first flight. Perhaps it was the way she had searched for the place that contained the oxygen mask when it was mentioned, or maybe it was the fact that not only was she the only person she saw holding the card that told about the plane exits, but she had been studying it intently. And she was positive her grand composure was slipping as the plane backed away from the terminal and began to taxi.

Grabbing her purse, she quickly pulled out a pack of gum and tore open the package. Myra had advised her to chew gum during takeoff and landing. She glanced at the man beside her and wasn't sure if he was looking at her or out the window. Trying to relieve her awkwardness, she offered him gum from the freshly opened pack.

"No, thanks. Already have some. I like bubble gum myself."

"Really," she replied. Tasting the mint of her own gum, she wondered how long it had been since she had chewed bubble gum.

The plane came to a stop, the engines roared, and Jenni said a quick prayer as the plane speeded up the runway and then lifted off the ground. Relaxing a bit and letting out a sigh, she realized that she had been gripping the armrests so hard her fingers were white. As the plane climbed higher, the landscape below took on the appearance of a patchwork quilt laid out beautifully below her. Highways and rivers divided neat sections of varied colors and designs.

The plane continued to climb and the river became a shiny ribbon winding around patterned pieces. The sight stirred her thoughts again. *How I wish my grandfather were here with me. I wouldn't be nervous or afraid with him. He would say something like, "God made the world, surely He can fly a plane."*

She smiled at the thought and remembered all the hot summer nights she and her grandfather sat in the squeaky old porch swing while Papa talked about Jesus. On Sundays they went to the little country church. It was there that Jenni gave her life to Christ when she was ten years old. Suddenly she felt tears stinging behind her eyes. She swallowed hard and blinked them back, wondering whom she would talk to when she needed guidance. Papa always made everything seem so simple. She could still hear him saying, "Darlin', if you ever find yourself wondering whether something is right or wrong, just ask yourself this question, 'Is this what Jesus would do?' That will usually give you your answer."

Jenni had tried to live by her grandfather's simple philosophy. She hoped the summer that lay ahead wouldn't present anything too difficult for that advice to sustain her.

Just then she felt a "bump" on the bottom of the plane and looked around cautiously. No one seemed to notice. She felt the man's blue eyes looking at her again, and she turned her head in his direction.

"Air currents," he said.

"What about air currents?" Jenni asked, wondering if he made a habit of answering questions that were never asked.

"The bumpiness you feel. They're air currents."

"Oh." Jenni relaxed and allowed a smile to cross her face.

"First flight?"

"Obvious, huh?"

"No, not really," he said. "Of course, I was a little concerned that the armrest wasn't going to make it through the takeoff." His blue eyes shone and a smile lit up his face.

"It really wasn't so bad as I expected," Jenni said, trying to gain some self-confidence.

"I'm Trey Maddox," he said, holding out his hand.

"Jenni Lawson." Trey's large hand engulfed Jenni's smaller one in a handshake, and she felt something inside that she couldn't explain. *Act sensibly*! she silently reprimanded herself. She didn't like the disconcerting attraction she felt toward the man beside her.

"You fly often?" Jenni asked, pulling her hand away and trying to make light conversation.

"Oh, I wouldn't say often. Couple of trips a year." Trey

settled himself comfortably in his chair then turned toward her again. "Are you from Oklahoma City?"

"No. I mean, yes. Yes, I–I'm from Oklahoma City."

Trey looked a little puzzled. "You sure?"

"I guess I'm just a little nervous. I thought you were going to ask where I was going, and when you didn't say Orlando, I had this terrible thought that I was on the wrong plane."

"So you're going to Orlando?"

"Well, actually, I'm going to Cocoa Beach." Jenni caught herself. Why was she telling this stranger where she was going? She warned herself to be more careful. That was one lesson she should take from Doug. He used to get irritated with her because she would carry on conversations with total strangers while they waited in lines at restaurants or other places. She decided it best to keep the attention on Trey. "And where are you from?"

"Well, my parents live in Oklahoma City, but I grew up in New Orleans, so take your pick."

"I'm prejudiced toward Oklahoma."

"It's nice enough, but I'm always ready to get home."

"Then where is home?" she asked, totally confused.

"Florida. That's where I work."

This sparked Jenni's interest. "Do you live near Orlando?"

"Actually," he said slowly with a smile, "I live in Cocoa Beach. And I am certainly looking forward to this summer."

Jenni felt a hot flush on her neck and cheeks. Trey was obviously enjoying her embarrassing moment. He leaned his chin on his hand while resting his elbow on the armrest, watching her with dancing blue eyes, a smile lighting up his handsome face. She was beginning to wonder if he ever quit smiling.

"What kind of work do you do, Mr. Maddox?" She thought being a little formal might discourage any friendly suggestions from him.

"Trey, call me Trey." He spoke his name slowly with a little melody to his voice. "I'm a speech pathologist."

"And you practice in Cocoa Beach?"

Trey drawled, "Yeah, you could say that."

"Meaning?"

"I see about eight clients right now." Something in his manner made Jenni wonder if he was teasing, but she decided it was simply his effervescent personality.

"You see only eight clients?"

"Right. But those eight are pretty special."

I'll bet they are, thought Jenni. *They must be as rich as Texas oil for you to be able to make a living by seeing only eight people.*

"What will you be doing in Cocoa Beach?" Trey asked.

Jenni paused then thought surely there wouldn't be any harm in telling him about her work since she had already told him where she was going. "I'll be working at a theater."

"You sing?"

"I dance."

Trey's smile broadened.

"I do ballet," she quickly added.

Trey laughed outright.

Jenni felt her face burn with anger. Seeing Trey's gaze rest on her long slender legs, she shifted in her seat but quickly lost her composure when the light came on to fasten seat belts and the plane took a sudden dip.

"What was that?" Jenni gasped, then she realized she had grabbed her seatmate's arm. "I'm sorry!" She couldn't believe what she had done.

"Hey, no problem."

Just at that moment a child tripped and fell in the aisle beside them. Trey quickly grabbed the frightened little boy. "Hey, tiger, you okay?"

A stewardess rushed to take the child. "Thank you. This is Brian's first trip alone and I'm having a hard time keeping him buckled in. Come on, Brian. We'd better do what the captain says."

The pilot was on the intercom instructing them to keep their seat belts fastened because of turbulence. Jenni looked out the window and prayed silently.

Trey's hand touched her arm lightly. "Hey, I'm sorry I teased you," he said seriously. "You're doing great for a first flight, especially in all this turbulence. I get uneasy in rough weather, too."

"Really?" She had a hard time believing anything would shake this man's confidence.

"Sure. Everyone does, but it usually doesn't last long."

She gave him a questioning look.

"Scout's honor." Trey raised three fingers.

Jenni smiled, actually believing what he said. Something about the gentle way he held the little boy had won her trust. "Well, I hope you're right because I don't think my stomach could take many dips and turns like we've been doing the last few minutes."

"Just put your mind on something else. Tell me about your dancing."

"Oh, I'd rather not."

"No, really, I'd like to know. I go to the theater anytime I get the opportunity."

"Really? Can you tell me what the Civic Theater is like in Cocoa Beach?"

"You mean you've never been there?"

"No. It's a sister company to the dance company I work for in Oklahoma, so that's how I got the job. My friend Myra works there, but I've never actually been to the theater. In fact, I've never even been to Florida."

"Oh, you'll like Florida. Everyone does."

"Have you lived there long?"

"About five years. Maybe I could show you around."

"Thanks, but I don't have any idea what my schedule will be like. And I'm sure Myra has plans to show me the sights." Jenni didn't want to encourage Trey. Even though she found him attractive and easy to talk to, she still didn't know the man. Besides, she didn't want to get involved in some summer romance. It hardly seemed fair to Doug. And after all, she was in Florida for one reason—to work.

The plane was moving smoothly again, so Jenni leaned back in her seat, closed her eyes, and tried to imagine what life in Cocoa Beach would be like. She was certain she would love the theater no matter how hard she had to work. Being a perfectionist when it came to dancing, she didn't worry about long hours of class or rehearsal.

The captain's voice came over the intercom. "Ladies and gentlemen, we are beginning our descent and should be arriving in Orlando on schedule. We hope you enjoyed your flight." There was a shuffle of papers and books as everyone put things away. A stewardess walked down the aisle collecting empty glasses and checking seat belts. Jenni looked out the window and saw a landscape far different from Oklahoma's. It was dotted with lakes and there were no neat borders like the mile intersections at home. She glanced over at Trey, who appeared to be asleep, eyes closed and arms folded across his chest.

There was a part of her that was sorry she wouldn't be seeing him again. Trey opened his eyes and Jenni felt embarrassed that he had caught her staring at him. She turned away quickly.

"Well, you're almost home," he drawled, sitting up straight in his seat.

"Just for the summer."

"You never know. Florida has a way of keeping people."

"I don't think so. My b—." Jenni caught herself before saying "boyfriend," then finished the sentence. "My mother would be beside herself if I didn't come home."

Jenni's ears began to pop at the change in altitude, and she felt tense at the thought of the landing.

Trey must have noticed. "Landing isn't bad," he said, turning toward her. "A lot like takeoff, except in reverse."

There was a bump of wheels and the plane raced down the runway before coming to a halt.

Trey smiled at Jenni. "Welcome to the Sunshine State."

two

Jenni looked around the waiting area for Myra, then heard her name called on the intercom. She stepped to the desk. "I'm Jenni Lawson."

"We have a message for you, Miss Lawson."

The message read, "Call Myra."

"Is there a problem?" Jenni turned to see Trey standing behind her. "I heard your name called and saw that no one met you."

"Uh. . .I don't know. I need to call my friend."

"I'll wait. You might need a ride." Trey took a seat near the phone.

Jenni called and found that Myra was having car problems.

"I can't pick you up, Jenni."

"Myra!"

"I'm sorry, but I don't know what to do."

Jenni tried to remain calm and think sensibly. "Is there a bus to Cocoa Beach?"

"I don't know."

"Look, Myra, you have to help me."

"But I don't know about the transportation system here."

Jenni's mind raced as she closed her eyes and rubbed her forehead with her free hand. Doug's words jumped into Jenni's consciousness. *Oh, stop,* she told herself. *Car problems don't make Myra unreliable.*

"Maybe I could rent a car," Jenni said more to herself than to Myra. She tried to put a light note to her voice that she didn't really feel. "Hey, don't worry, I'll manage." She hung up the phone and turned to find Trey beside her.

"I didn't mean to eavesdrop, but I'll be glad to give you a ride."

"No, I wouldn't want to bother you." It was against her better judgment to ride with someone she had met only hours earlier on a plane.

"It's no bother. I'm headed there anyway."

"That's really not necessary," Jenni replied curtly. She wanted to assert her independence, then realized she had none to assert at the moment. "I. . .I appreciate your offer for a ride, but I'd prefer to rent a car. With mine in the garage, I might need one for a while anyway."

"I thought it was your friend's car."

"She was picking me up in it. She and a friend drove it down for me."

Trey looked at her quizzically.

"It's a long story. Well, not really. Myra is from Oklahoma City, too, and we were going to drive down together. But when my grand—" Jenni paused and looked away. It was too soon to talk about her grandfather. "Well, something happened, so Myra drove the car and I flew."

Trey was watching her intently, and she wondered why she was explaining all this to someone who was little more than a stranger. She flashed a big smile. "So, there you have it. I think I'll probably need a rental."

Trey nodded his head, and Jenni knew he must think she was half crazy. "Whatever you say. I'll help you find one."

"That's not necessary," she said. Trey turned, a solemn expression replacing the usual smile. "Of course, if you happen to know where a rental office is, I suppose it would be helpful." Trey accepted her unspoken truce and, taking her arm, guided her through the crowds of people. As they walked side by side through the terminal, Trey didn't seem quite so tall as he had in the plane, but he still towered above Jenni's five-feet-six inches.

After renting a car, Trey helped collect her bags, then asked her to wait while he went to the parking garage for his own car. "You might as well follow me from the airport and out of Orlando."

"Trey, this really isn't necessary. I'm sure I can make it just fine with a good map."

"I'm sure you can, too, but I'd feel better if I saw you safely to Cocoa Beach."

"Just like a big brother, huh?" Seeing the look in Trey's eyes, she was immediately sorry she had made such a statement.

"Well, I can't say I feel brotherly toward you—"

"Never mind. I'll wait. Just get your car, please." She familiarized herself with the rental car and map while waiting, all the while wondering if following Trey was a good idea.

A red Corvette drove up slowly and Jenni buckled her seat belt and turned on the ignition, somehow knowing Trey would be driving such a car. But the car kept going while a white van with ugly rust spots stopped in front of her. Trey jumped out of the van and ran over to her. *Well, so much for the sports car,* she thought. She tried not to look surprised but obviously did not succeed, judging from Trey's comment.

"I know. Not much to look at. That's why I feel safe leaving it in the parking garage while I'm gone."

"Oh. . .no," Jenni stammered. "It's fine."

"Well, it runs great and the kids love it when we take little trips with them."

Jenni felt her mouth drop open. Kids! He had kids? Was he married? Jenni had just assumed, since he wore no wedding band. . .but then lots of men didn't wear wedding bands. But hadn't he asked to show her around? Surely she hadn't imagined that. No, she was certain she had not. And he had definitely been attentive toward her. Suddenly she was angry at Trey for deceiving her; then she caught herself. *Maybe he's a single father,* she thought to herself. *That's possible, even probable*. But she wanted to find out.

"You actually take trips in that," she motioned toward the van, "with children?"

"Well, we just go to the beach. But the kids love it. Besides, there are too many to take in the car."

"How many children are there?"

"Eight."

"Eight! Eight children?" Jenni heard her voice rise in surprise.

"Hey, I'm good with kids. Besides, Anne usually goes along, too."

Anne? Now he's going to tell me about his wife? No, thank you. "Trey, I really need to be on my way to Cocoa Beach. If you will excuse me." Jenni started to roll up the window, but Trey grabbed it.

"Wait, wait, wait. Don't get in such a hurry." He leaned inside the window and took the map from her lap. "Just follow me, but if by chance we get separated, take the exit I've marked."

"I'm sure I'll be fine." Jenni just wanted to get to the apartment and put Trey Maddox out of her mind forever.

"Here." Trey dumped a handful of change in her lap. "Lots of tolls between here and Cocoa Beach." Jenni opened her mouth to protest, but Trey was already bounding off to the old white van. He climbed inside and waved. She followed, knowing there was little else she could do at the moment.

As she drove she absorbed the scenery around her, surprised at the sparse palm trees and tropical foliage. Somehow she had expected all of Florida to be a tropical paradise. She tried to think about Cocoa Beach and the theater, but Trey kept coming to her mind. He had a wife and children! *And I almost trusted him,* she thought.

"Jenni, how could you be so stupid?" she reprimanded herself aloud. "When will you learn not to trust everyone you meet?" She knew that Doug would be glad to say "I told you so," if he knew, but this would be one incident that he would never know of. She sighed aloud, feeling a little guilty that the thought of Doug caused no feelings of loneliness at all.

Suddenly she was crossing the causeway that led to Merritt Island and Cocoa Beach. Jenni's excitement began to mount. The palm trees were abundant and the ocean was barely off Main Street.

Directly in front of her, Trey put his arm out of the van and motioned her over to a service station. Jenni pulled her car in behind the van, and Trey trotted back to her car. "What's the address?"

"Oh, I guess that would be helpful, wouldn't it?" Jenni dug into her purse for the address, then handed it to Trey. "I hope you know where this is. I didn't think to ask Myra for directions."

Trey gave a big smile. "I'm sure I can find it."

True to his word, they drove up to a two-story white structure with stairs in the middle and at each end of the building. A veranda with wrought-iron railing stretched along the front of both floors. Flowers were abundant and palm trees surrounded the building. As soon as she got out of the car, Jenni saw Myra wave to her from the first apartment on the second floor. Trey helped carry her luggage up the stairs and into the apartment while Myra squealed and grabbed Jenni in a hug.

"Myra, this is Trey Maddox," she said as they stepped inside the apartment. "This is my roommate, Myra Johnson."

"Let me get you a glass of iced tea," Myra said as she took one of the smaller bags from Trey's hand.

"No, thanks," he said with a smile that Jenni already found familiar as he set her luggage in the middle of the modest-sized living room. "I need to get home. Bye, Jenni. I hope we'll be seeing each other again real soon."

Jenni's cheeks flushed. "Good-bye, Trey. Thanks for your help."

Myra closed the door to the apartment as Jenni sank into an overstuffed chair by a window looking out to the parking lot.

"Jenni, I'm so glad you're finally here." Myra was bursting with excitement. "And I think I did you a favor by not showing up at the airport." She looked out the window with Jenni. "That is one good-looking guy."

"He's married."

"Married? He didn't talk like he was married. I got the impression he wanted to see you again."

"He told me about Anne and the children."

"He has children?"

"Yep. Eight!"

"Eight children? Oh, Jenni, no one has eight children anymore, especially someone as young as he is."

"Myra, he told me the kids liked the van, if you can believe that, and loved to go to the beach. When I asked how many, he said 'eight.' "

"Wow! Must be twins, wouldn't you say?"

"Oh, I don't know and I don't care. Come on, show me the apartment." Jenni stood up to take the tour but took one quick glance out the window as Trey's van disappeared from the parking lot.

❧

In the few days that Jenni had been in town, Myra had shown her most of Cocoa Beach, along with her favorite restaurants and places to shop. They had walked to the beach, which was only a couple of blocks from the apartment, and today they were going to Disney World. Jenni was taking full advantage of the few days she had free before starting work on Monday.

The phone rang and Myra talked for a while then came into the kitchen where Jenni was drinking orange juice and reading the newspaper.

"Jenni, I'm going to have to cancel on Disney World today. One of the girls is sick and I need to fill in for her. I'm really sorry."

"Oh, don't worry about it. We'll go another time. After all, we've got the whole summer." Jenni smiled, but inside she was disappointed. She hated the thought of spending the whole day alone.

"Listen, I hate to leave you like this. You want to come to the studio?"

"No, you have work to do. I'll probably just go for a walk. Maybe I'll go to the beach and start my tan."

"Okay, I'd better run. Don't stay out in the sun too long and don't wait up for me. It may be late tonight when I get in."

"Yes, little mother." Jenni smiled as she saw Myra off, locking the door behind her. She walked back to the bedroom to get her bathing suit, but before she could change from her red short set she heard a knock on the door. *Myra must have forgotten something,* she thought as she ran to the living room. She opened the door to find Trey leaning against the doorjamb, dressed in navy walking shorts and a white knit shirt.

"What are you doing here?" Jenni asked abruptly.

"I just thought I'd drop by and see if you were settled in. I noticed you got your car out of the garage." He nodded toward the parking area.

"How would you know if my car is out of the garage?"

"Oklahoma license plate. Only one out there." He gave a broad smile.

Jenni stood staring at him.

"May I come in?"

"I suppose." Jenni stepped away from the door.

Trey stepped into the apartment and walked over to the ceiling fan. He pulled the chain, fumbled with a button, then motioned toward the wall. "Turn that switch on, will you?"

Jenni jammed her fists against her hips and walked over to confront him. "What do you think you are doing?"

"Fixing your ceiling fan. You are having problems with it, aren't you?"

"And how would you know that?"

"Because I'm your handy-dandy fix-it man." He smiled, seeming to enjoy her confusion.

"You know, I don't really like you and I'd prefer not to have this conversation at all. But since you are here, handy-dandy whoever, I might remind you that you told me you were a speech pathologist."

"I am. Try that switch," he said without looking away from the fan.

Jenni turned on the switch and the fan began to turn. "How did you do that?" she asked, completely irritated that he had actually fixed the fan.

"Too complicated to explain."

Jenni was not amused. "Would you please tell me why a speech pathologist is fixing my fan?" Her voice was rising in anger.

"Because my aunt is your landlady and I help her with odd jobs during the summers." Trey gave his ear-to-ear smile.

"When do you start work?"

"Monday," she said, standing in the middle of the room, arms folded across her chest. "Not that it's any of your business."

"Of course it's my business. That means you have today free. I thought we would go to Disney World."

"You thought *what*?" Jenni couldn't keep the shock from her voice.

"Disney World. You know, Mickey Mouse, Donald Duck, Goofy—"

"Aren't you assuming an awful lot?"

"Why? Do you have plans?"

"Well. . .yes. . .sort of. I mean, yes, I do."

"So, what are they?"

"That's none of your business!"

"That's true, but I personally don't think you have any real plans." He walked over to face her. "You're a very poor liar."

Jenni's anger erupted. "You're one to talk about lying. I think you could stand to tell the truth more often."

"What do you mean?"

"Your wife, that's what I mean. Why didn't you tell me you were married?" The words were out before Jenni realized what she was saying.

"Married? Where in the thunder did you get an idea like that? I've never been married in my life."

"You haven't? I mean, you're not?"

"No!"

"Oh, I don't believe you." She took a step backward. It bothered her to be so close to Trey. "Of course you would say that."

"Why should I lie about that? What made you think I was married anyway?"

"Well. . .the children. You said you had eight children."

"What?" Trey exclaimed.

"You said you and Anne take them to the beach in the old van that you had at the airport."

"Oh, no." Trey slapped his hand to his forehead then sat

down on the sofa and laughed while Jenni watched in silence.

"Oh, Jenni, I can't believe you thought I had eight kids." He began to laugh again.

Jenni felt the color rising in her neck and cheeks. Had she really made a mistake? But who were Anne and the children? She couldn't decide if she was angry or pleased.

Trey stood up and walked toward her. "I'm sorry for laughing. But eight kids?"

"But you said—"

"I know," he said, waving a hand to stop her speech. "I just forgot that you didn't know that much about me. Remember I told you I was a speech pathologist?"

"Yes."

"The eight children are the kids I teach."

"Teach? You mean in school?"

"Yes, I'm a speech pathologist in the public schools, and this summer I'm working with a group of developmentally disabled children—eight of them!"

Jenni felt embarrassed but also relieved. She couldn't count how many times she had thought of Trey and his smile the last few days. "And Anne?" she asked boldly.

"The physical therapist." Trey smiled and took hold of her hand.

"Boy, do I feel silly. I don't know what to say."

"Just say you'll go to Disney World with me."

Jenni caught her lower lip between her teeth, contemplating a day with Trey. "Actually, that's where Myra and I were going when she was called to work."

"Then what are we waiting for? Oh, and just in case you're worried about transportation, I'm driving my Blazer instead of the old van and your landlady will definitely vouch for my character."

Jenni finally smiled. "In that case, I'm ready," she said, surprised by her own quick response.

three

Making himself the official guide, Trey decided they would see the Magic Kingdom on Jenni's first visit to Disney World. When they boarded the monorail at the gate, Jenni was as excited as a six-year-old.

Standing at the entrance to Main Street, Jenni held a hand up to shield her sun-shaded eyes and look around. There were buildings everywhere. Restaurants and souvenir shops surrounded her, and Cinderella's castle towered at the end of Main Street with paths going in all directions. The sun was hot overhead and Jenni was glad she had used plenty of sunscreen. She dug out a cap from her fanny pack and pulled her ponytail through the back. "I can't believe how big this place is," she said to Trey, giving an encompassing gesture with her hands. "We'll never see all of it."

"That's the fun of it. Always something to come back to see." Trey took off his sunglasses and let them fall loosely to his chest, securely attached to a cord around his neck. "We are right here," he said, pointing to a place on the map. "We'll take the train later because we want to be at the depot for the afternoon parade." He pointed toward the depot. "That's the best place to see everything." Jenni nodded. "Okay, let's start with one of my favorite rides. I know you're going to like it." Trey beamed. He was truly enjoying his role as tour guide.

"I'm ready," Jenni said, feeling certain they were headed for a log flume ride or something similar. Instead, she found herself boarding a boat to the Small World ride. She welcomed the shade and the cool air of the water canal as the boat moved slowly through a world of marionettes singing and dancing to the music, "It's a Small World." Mexican dancers and mariachi bands gave a Spanish flavor to the music, then Swiss marionettes yodeled as goats grazed in meadows. Around each bend of the winding water canal a new sight and sound awaited her. Flying carpets with veiled marionettes, can-can dancers, wooden drummers, then hula girls and surfers. Jenni loved the ride and wondered how Trey could have known she would enjoy something like this so much. She also wondered why she felt a tingle of excitement every time his arm brushed against hers. Jenni gave her heart a little warning. *This is no time to get romantic. The summer is reserved for work*, she reminded herself.

The ride came to an end and they stepped back into the hot Florida sun.

"That was beautiful."

"I knew you'd like it."

But how did you know? she wanted to ask.

They walked together hand in hand, stopping occasionally to look through souvenir shops and cool off a bit, or to decide whether they wanted to wait in a long line for a particular ride.

"Let's get something to eat," Trey said.

"Sounds good."

"Let's see, we're in Tomorrow Land; maybe we could find space burgers or something like that."

They sat at an outside table in a crowded eating area. Jenni bowed her head and said a silent prayer of thanks before eating. Trey was staring at her when she raised her head.

"Do you always do that?" he asked.

"Yes, why?"

"Just wondered. Most people just pray at family dinners and that sort of thing."

"I believe God expects me to be as thankful for a hamburger as a turkey dinner."

"Guess you're right."

After eating, Jenni slipped off her shoes and massaged her feet before lacing on her sneakers again.

"Think you're going to make it through the whole park?"

"Sure. I just need to take a break now and then. Ballet is really hard on the feet."

"We can manage that. You'll be sitting during the parade at three, then there's a great musical program about six."

"Boy, you have this down to a science, don't you?" Jenni laughed.

"You have to have a plan. Otherwise you just wander around. It's so big it sometimes overwhelms first-time visitors."

"I believe it. I don't think I have ever seen so many people in one place. And I know I've heard at least three different languages spoken, maybe more."

"You know what's really funny, though? As big as this place is, I hardly ever come out here without seeing someone I know."

"Sounds impossible, but I knew a woman in Oklahoma who said she actually ran into her child's pediatrician at Disney World."

About that time a woman with a child, who looked to be about four or five years old, walked by. The little girl suddenly stopped and threw her arms around Trey's neck.

"Chrissy! Are you having fun?" Trey picked up the child and hugged her. The dark-haired little girl nodded her head, her ponytail bobbing, but she didn't speak.

"Didn't I tell you I always see someone I know?" he said to Jenni as he introduced her to the child and her foster parent. "Chrissy, this is my friend, Jenni. Can you tell her 'hi'?" Chrissy smiled but still said nothing, keeping her arms wrapped tightly around Trey's neck. Her brown eyes had a slight upward tilt and her smile made them twinkle, reminding Jenni of the pretty animated children she had seen on the Small World ride. Chrissy gave Trey one last hug before leaving but never spoke a word.

Trey and Jenni finished their soft drinks, then walked along a bridge overflowing with red and white petunias. Trailing pink geraniums hung from baskets.

"You really like children, don't you?" Jenni asked, thinking about the little girl.

"Yeah, I love working with them. Especially these kids."

"Is Chrissy one of the children you teach?"

"Yes. In fact, I've had Chrissy all year."

"Didn't you say they were handicapped or something?"

"Developmentally disabled is the term we use."

"Is that why Chrissy didn't speak?"

Trey tilted his head up a bit, as if he was thinking, then led her to a bench under an umbrella. Tall red cannas bloomed behind them. "Yes and no," he finally said as they sat down.

"What kind of an answer is that?"

"An evasive one, I guess. But I can't give you an exact reason why Chrissy doesn't speak. Certainly her disability is a contributing factor, but how much, I don't know. Chrissy has Down syndrome."

"What's that?"

"Children with Down syndrome have an extra chromosome which causes developmental delays. It's usually mild and they lead fairly normal lives."

"Do any of them talk?"

"Oh, sure," Trey said, seeming amused by the question. "In fact, most of them speak quite well with a little speech therapy. Chrissy's speech, or I should say lack of speech, is an exception. That's why I answered the way I did. I don't know that her disability has as much to do with her speech problem as her emotional state. She was taken out of an abusive home and put in foster care."

Jenni didn't respond.

"Have you ever worked with disabled people?"

"Me?" Jenni was astonished that he would ask such a question.

"Yeah. I thought maybe you might have helped through your church or something."

"No. In fact, I've never been around them."

"Them?"

"People with disabilities." Jenni found Trey's enthusiasm

for the children admirable, but the conversation was uncomfortable for her. She now knew more about disabled people than she had ever known and had little desire to know more.

Trey ended the conversation abruptly. He stood up, took her hand, and pulled her up from the bench. "Come on, let's head to Space Mountain. Since it's lunchtime, maybe the line won't be so long."

"What's Space Mountain?"

Trey chuckled. "Probably one of the most popular rides at Disney World."

"Then let's go." She liked all rides except roller coasters, and after her incessant screaming during the dark roller coaster ride called Space Mountain, she was certain that Trey also knew her particular preferences.

At midafternoon they rode the train to the Main Street entrance and watched the colorful parade from the second-story depot. They ate ice cream bars while the two-story floats glided by and costumed dancers filled the streets. It was so easy to be caught up in the excitement, and Jenni felt she had known Trey forever as she fulfilled childhood fantasies that she never seemed to have time for because of her rigorous dance schedule. Earlier, while riding the carousel, she had thought of Doug and was certain he would think a carousel ride was silly for an adult.

Night came and they had seen only a fraction of the sights. They watched the glittering light parade, then fireworks exploded overhead as they took the ferryboat away from the island.

On the way home, Jenni wondered if she would ever have another day like this one. Arriving at the apartment, she was glad to find that Myra was still gone. She needed some time to think. She was puzzled about her feelings for Trey, especially since she had left Doug only days ago. Then there was his reaction to her prayer. Did he share her Christian beliefs? She didn't want to judge his actions, having known lots of people who were uncomfortable praying in public. But Trey seemed more curious than uncomfortable.

Trey opened the car door for Jenni, and they walked up the stairs and to her door together. Cool, salty ocean breezes mixed with the strong, sweet fragrances of jasmine and gardenia. Trey took Jenni's hand as they stood under the soft light of the veranda, then kissed her lightly on the cheek. "Good night, Jenni. I had a great time today." He leaned close to her ear and whispered mischievously, "Especially without my wife and eight kids."

Jenni gave him a playful swat on the arm and smiled. "I enjoyed it, too. I never had much time for recreation. Seems like I was always dancing."

"Well, we'll just have to change that." Trey winked and walked away.

I don't think so, Jenni thought as she let herself into the apartment. Locking the door behind her, she walked over to the window in the dark, snuggled down in the big, overstuffed chair, and watched the lights of Trey's car disappear into the night. "No, I don't think that would be at all wise," she said aloud with a tinge of disappointment.

four

Jenni's stomach began to churn as she and Myra pulled into the parking area of the theater. "Maybe you'd better go on inside," Jenni said. "I think I'm going to be sick."

"I've never seen you like this. Why are you so nervous? You know Mr. Overstreet wouldn't have recommended you if he didn't think you could do the job."

"But Mr. Overstreet is in Oklahoma, not here."

"Let's go inside. You'll be fine."

Jenni wasn't so sure. Even outside in the hot sunshine, her hands were as cold as ice. Inside, doubts overwhelmed her as she looked around at the studio and the other performers. What if she couldn't do the dance variations? What if she just wasn't good enough for the job? What if. . .what if. . .

After pinning her hair into a bun and changing shoes, she began some warm-up exercises at the *barre*. Her strong, slender legs and long arms were certainly an asset to ballet, but she had worked hard since she was five years old to perfect her dance to what it was today.

While she was doing leg stretches, a tall, attractive woman whom Jenni guessed to be in her mid-forties approached her. She had flawless olive skin and dark medium-length hair pulled to one side. She asked Jenni about her previous work and told her what was expected of her.

"You will have class from ten to eleven-thirty Monday through Thursday and rehearsal each afternoon. Performances are on Friday and Saturday nights, so you'll have a different schedule on those days. I'm hoping you will be able to eventually do a solo performance. But of course that depends on how hard you work."

Jenni nodded with each statement. Her mouth was dry and her hands shaky.

"Your director, Miles Overstreet, gave you an excellent recommendation, so I'll expect to see that excellence. We're glad to have you with us."

Knowing she should say something, Jenni finally stammered, "Thank you. I'll do my best."

"I'm certain you will. Miles and I have been friends for years. He's never sent me a bad performer yet." The woman smiled and walked away, and Jenni closed her eyes and let out a long sigh. She wanted to shout, "Yes, yes, I'll work hard and I'll make it to a solo." She was so exuberant she had a hard time going back to exercises. Myra glanced her way and gave an "okay" sign and a big smile. Jenni was now more determined than ever to do her best work in Florida.

By the end of the week she was feeling comfortable with the other dancers and was working on a *pas de deux* with her partner when Trey showed up at the studio. A little embarrassed that he should visit her at work, Jenni quickly ran over to the door to see what he wanted.

"Listen, I'm sorry about interrupting you like this, but I wanted to ask you something."

"I'm sure it's okay," she said, a little short of breath.

Trey reached over and wiped her damp forehead. Jenni's pulse quickened and she wondered what she must look like with no makeup and her skin shiny with perspiration.

"What did you want to ask me?" Her breath came more evenly now.

"Some friends asked me to meet them for dinner tonight. I'd like for you to go with me. I know it's short notice, but they just called this morning."

Jenni hesitated. Part of her wanted to be with Trey, and part of her didn't want to get involved. "I'm not sure when I'll be through. I wouldn't want to make you wait."

"I don't think that would be a problem. I'm not meeting them until eight."

Something in his pleading blue eyes melted her resolve and she accepted the invitation. "I. . .I guess I could do it then. Sure. It sounds wonderful." Jenni smiled and tried to put her reservations out of her mind. She enjoyed Trey's company, so why shouldn't she go? She was glad there was no onc to answer that question. She knew it herself.

"Great. I'll pick you up a little after seven." He reached up and brushed a strand of hair away from her face, then turned to leave. Jenni felt that same electric sensation that she had felt at Disney World.

"Oh, Trey," Jenni called and ran over to him. "What should I wear?"

"It's a dress-up thing, but I kind of like the way you look right now." He stood back to admire her in her black leotard, tights, and shorts.

"Oh, go on. You're no help."

Jenni glanced around as she went back to work, wondering if anyone had been watching. But the others were involved in their own dance variations. The rest of the day went slowly and she found it a little more difficult to concentrate knowing she would be seeing Trey tonight. Her resolution to have no summer romance was working about as well as most of her New Year's resolutions.

❧

Dressed in white slacks and a navy sports coat, Trey looked as if he belonged on some luxury yacht. As he stepped into the apartment, Jenni again noticed his deep bronze tan and sun-bleached hair. Her heart skipped a beat when he flashed a bright smile and looked at her with sky blue eyes. He reached out and took her hand, turning her around in a manner of showing his approval of how she looked.

"I don't know what kind of show they have planned for the evening, but I have a feeling when you walk into the room, you'll be the one onstage. Hm-mm, you are beautiful!"

Jenni smiled at his approval. She had taken great pains to dress just right for the evening. It had taken her thirty minutes just to decide what to wear, then at the last minute she changed her mind and took off the teal silk dress and put on the deep purple dinner dress she was now wearing. The small spaghetti straps on the shoulders showed off her smooth skin, and the soft folds of the skirt clung to the contours of her body.

Her dark hair was piled on top of her head, while wispy tendrils fell onto her neck and around her face.

The covered walkway that led from the parking area to the restaurant was flanked on one side with a waterfall that ran into a pool under the walkway, then sprayed into a fountain on the other side. Large red hibiscus blossomed along the walkway.

"Looks exclusive," Jenni said.

"If you mean expensive, yes, it is. But don't worry. They won't make you wash dishes if we can't pay. You can dance instead."

"Do your friends teach, too?"

"No, John's a speech pathologist, but in private practice."

Jenni took hold of Trey's arm as they walked into the restaurant. "Don't worry. You'll like them," he said, seeming to read her mind.

The waiter seated them at a table beside a glass wall overlooking tropical gardens. Jenni smiled pleasantly through introductions to John and Cindy. Both appeared to be in their late twenties or early thirties. John was of medium height and build, not nearly so tall as Trey, and had dark hair. He seemed reserved, but compared to Trey, most people seemed reserved. Cindy had strawberry blond hair, a beautiful smile, and wore a white silk dress. Jenni liked her immediately.

"We could hardly wait to meet you," Cindy said. "All we've heard from Trey the last few days is 'Jenni.' "

Feeling a flush of color rising to her neck and face, she looked toward Trey, assuming the statement would embarrass him. But instead he seemed thoroughly pleased.

"Yes, we decided to make a dinner date to see if you were real," John said with dry humor. "Knowing Trey as we do, we couldn't believe anyone with all the qualities he described would possibly be interested in him. But I see for once he was completely truthful." John smiled.

Jenni murmured a low thank you, relieved to have the conversation interrupted by a waiter with salads and fruit. She felt Trey's gaze on her when she bowed her head to pray, and he was still watching when she lifted her head. She unfolded the white linen napkin and placed it on her lap. "This pineapple is delicious," she said, glancing at Trey, but he was now talking to John.

"The fresh fruit is one of the things I like about Florida," Cindy said.

The conversation jumped from one thing to another throughout the meal of prime rib and seafood, then finally rested on Trey's work. It seemed that all who knew him knew how dedicated he was to his "kids."

"You know, if I could just get people to realize what potential these kids have. They can mainstream into school, jobs, everywhere, if people will just give them the opportunity."

John picked up his water goblet. "Well, I certainly think you've done your share for them."

"I don't know," Trey said. "You see, with some of them, speech is the main thing holding them back. They can't communicate and that's frustrating. If I could just find the key to unlock what's inside of them, I think the world would be shocked."

Jenni shifted uneasily in her chair. Why did these conversations bother her? She looked around the room full of diners. A young couple sitting beside them never seemed to take their eyes off each other. Jenni wondered if they were newlyweds. An older couple sat to their left, looking very distinguished and comfortable. Jenni caught herself and looked back at her dining companions, wondering if anyone noticed her discomfort with the discussion.

The waiter brought chocolate marble cheesecake with coffee and the conversation changed. The evening seemed to slip away.

"I liked John and Cindy," Jenni said on the way back to her apartment.

"I knew you would. They've listened to a lot of my frustrations, as you saw tonight."

"At the risk of sounding like a cliché, isn't that what friends are for?"

"I suppose. But good friends, like John and Cindy, are hard to come by."

"I know," Jenni said, wondering if Trey would place her in his category of good friends.

"Hey, let's get off this philosophical business and talk about you," Trey said.

"Me? Huh-uh! There's nothing interesting about me."

Trey pulled into the parking area to Jenni's apartment, stopped the car near a bright pole light, and turned off the engine. He turned to Jenni. "I disagree. I think you're the most interesting person I've ever met."

"Well, there is one thing we should talk about."

"Which is?"

"Maybe you shouldn't ask me to dinner again if it bothers you to see me pray before meals."

"I think I can handle that. Actually, I respect your convictions, just don't happen to agree with them."

"Well. . .you see, that's a problem for me."

"Why is that? I said I respect your convictions."

"Right. But you don't agree them. Why?"

Trey was silent for a while. "I think we should talk about that some other time." He reached over and took hold of Jenni's hand and looked deep into her eyes, the most serious Jenni had ever seen him.

She felt her heart speed up and a sort of bubbly feeling well up deep inside her. In all the months she and Doug dated, she had never felt anything like this. Why was she allowing this to happen? What if she actually fell in love? *Oh, Jenni, be careful,* she told herself.

Suddenly Trey dropped her hand, got out of the car, and walked over to Jenni's side. As she stepped out, Trey's arms circled around her, pulling her to him. He kissed her gently, and Jenni surprised herself by responding to his kiss.

Suddenly he pulled himself away and said something that shocked her. "Jenni, it would be so easy to fall in love with you." Without another word he took hold of her arm and walked her to the door of the apartment.

five

After four weeks Cocoa Beach felt like home. Jenni was sitting in the middle of the living room floor sewing ribbons on her pointe shoes when someone knocked at the door.

"Who is it?" she called without getting up.

"The IRS."

"Come in, Trey."

"Can't fool you, huh?" He sat down on the sofa. "What are you doing?"

"Sewing ribbons on my shoes."

"Well, I can see that, but why?"

"You think you could keep one of these on without tying it?" She threw a shoe into his lap.

"Good grief. You could use this for a weapon." He patted the hard toes of the shoe on his hand, then held it by the pink ribbons. "You did a good job."

"I've sewed enough ribbons on shoes to be an expert by now."

"I thought we were going to Epcot tonight." He tossed the shoe back to Jenni.

"We are. I just wanted to have my shoes ready for the performance Friday night. Myra says the laser light show is really pretty."

"You'll never know if you keep sewing ribbons, will you?"

She jumped up from the floor and threw her shoes onto the coffee table. "I'm ready. I'm ready."

Three hours later they sat under an umbrella by the lagoon, feeding ducks.

"I had no idea Epcot was so big. I wish we had enough time to walk through all the countries. Everything seems so authentic," Jenni said.

"Which country is your favorite so far?"

"Hmm, I love the music in Mexico, but the folk dancing was great in Germany. The food was good in the United Kingdom, and—"

"Never mind. I'm sorry I asked. Come on." He took her hand and pulled her to her feet. "We've got to get to the Secret Park."

"What's the Secret Park?"

"The best place to watch the laser light show."

They took a path off the main thoroughfare between the United Kingdom and France and came to a small circular area beside the lagoon. The benches were full, so they sat on the ground.

"Looks like the Secret Park isn't much of a secret," Jenni said, leaning back against Trey.

The colorful laser lights pierced the darkness, cutting across the lagoon to the refrains of Bach, Beethoven, and other classical artists. A different country lit up with each refrain.

"Isn't it beautiful?"

Trey didn't answer. He pulled her closer to him and Jenni snuggled into his arms, feeling warm, protected, and loved. *How can I feel so loved one moment and so confused another?* she asked herself. Over the past few weeks she had tried to have several conversations with Trey about her faith, and even though he continued to deny having faith in God, there was something about his respect and acceptance of her own faith that contradicted everything he said. Jenni closed her eyes and listened to strains of Beethoven.

"You know, I've danced to some of this music lots of times." She tilted her head up while leaning against his shoulder, smelling the musk of his cologne. Yawning, she rested her head back on his shoulder.

"Looks like you may sleep through the music this time."

"I'm sorry," Jenni laughed. "I promise I won't go to sleep. I'm just a little tired."

"We can leave."

"No! I want to see the fireworks. Besides, I don't have class tomorrow morning so I can sleep late."

"Since when do you get off on Thursdays?"

"Just tomorrow. They have a gas leak or something so no one can be in the building. The director is furious, but I'm thrilled. I have been working so hard on my solo that I can use the rest."

The fireworks exploded in the black sky, lighting up the lagoon below. Almost in unison the crowd of people "ahhed" over every burst of color.

On the hour-long drive back to Cocoa Beach, Jenni dropped off to sleep. Then all at once Trey was gently shaking her arm.

"Wake up, sweetheart. You're home."

"Oh, Trey, I'm sorry. I can't believe I fell asleep. What time is it?"

"Time for you to get upstairs and go to bed." He walked her to the door and gave her a gentle good-night kiss.

As she crawled into bed, Jenni saw a letter from Doug on the nightstand. A little sigh escaped her. "Why now? Why can't I just enjoy this night without feeling guilty?" she asked aloud. It seemed that each of Doug's letters was more intense about her coming home and their future. She wasn't sure what to do. Maybe she should just write and say, "I've met someone else." But that hardly seemed proper. Jenni yawned. *I'll write and tell him soon,* she promised herself and turned off the light.

❧

The phone was ringing when she stepped out of the shower. She grabbed her robe and ran to answer it.

"Trey? Why aren't you working?"

"I am, but I thought you might meet me for lunch."

"Any particular reason?" Glad she had grabbed the cordless phone, Jenni walked back into the bathroom.

"Hey, I'm getting worried. You're beginning to read my mind."

"So I'm right. You have an ulterior motive." Looking into the mirror, she found herself smiling. She took the pins out of her hair and let it fall loose.

"My main motive is wanting to see you, but I have to admit there is something I want to discuss with you."

"What?"

"Come to lunch and find out."

"Okay, I'll be there. Wait, where am I going to be? I hope it's not that little hamburger place you talk about."

"That's it! It's close and I don't have much time. Be adventuresome and try it."

"Oh, all right. I'll meet you at noon."

Jenni hung up the phone, wondering what he wanted to talk about.

Trey was waiting when she arrived at the restaurant.

"The food must be wonderful," she said, looking around at the room full of people.

"Well, it's not just your basic greasy hamburger place. It's your *deluxe* greasy hamburger. Come on, let's order," he said, ushering her toward a line of people.

"You mean I can't sit down?"

"After you order you can sit down, if you can find a table."

"Why do you come here?" Jenni asked, wrinkling her nose a bit as she looked around the room. She knew her clothes and hair would smell like hamburgers and French fries when she left.

"It's close and the food is good. You'll see."

They found a table toward the back, just cleared of dirty dishes. Jenni smiled across the table at Trey and toyed with the small packages of sugar, hoping she didn't appear too anxious to hear his news.

"I guess you're wondering what I wanted to ask you."

"I admit I'm a little curious," she said.

"Well, it's just an idea I have."

"About what?"

"About you."

"Me?"

"Actually, I've thought about it for a good while but didn't know whether I should ask you."

"Ask me what?" Jenni's curiosity had peaked.

"Well, I wondered if you—"

"Trey Maddox." The voice blared from a microphone. "Your order is ready."

"I'll be right back." Trey walked to the counter to get the order while Jenni waited impatiently.

"This must be yours." Trey handed Jenni a plate of cottage cheese and fruit. "I didn't even know they served stuff like that here." He set a hamburger and French fries at his own place and took a big bite.

"You were going to ask me something," Jenni said before beginning her meal.

"Right." Trey wiped his mouth with a napkin. "Like I said, I've thought about it before, but. . .well, what I wondered is if you might have a little free time to work with the kids at school."

Jenni frowned a little. "Doing what?"

"Teaching them to dance."

"Are we talking about the children you teach—the handicapped children?" Jenni asked, feeling her apprehension mount.

"Right." Trey dabbed some French fries in ketchup and offered them to Jenni.

"No, thanks."

"Well, what do you think?"

"I think you're going to die of a heart attack eating that greasy stuff."

"You know what I'm talking about." Trey wiped his mouth with his napkin, wadded it up, and dropped it in his French fry basket. He propped elbows on the table and put his fists under his chin, staring at her.

"Sorry, but no." Jenni didn't look at him.

"No? Just like that? Don't you want to think about it?"

"Hi, Trey." A young woman wearing a little red hat and apron stood beside the table carrying an empty tray and dirty dishcloth.

"Oh, hi, Jamie. Working hard?"

"The usual noon rush," she said, looking at Jenni. She walked to the table next to them and began clearing the dishes, clanging the glasses and plates together.

Trey turned back to Jenni and looked at her quizzically.

"I can't teach those children," Jenni spoke softly.

"What? I can't hear you."

Jenni raised her voice a little. "I said, I can't teach those children." She placed her napkin on the table beside her plate of half-finished food.

"Why?"

"Why?" Jenni repeated. "Because I'm not a teacher."

"So? You certainly know how to dance."

"But that's different."

"No, it isn't."

"Yes, it is." She pushed her hair away from her face with an impatient gesture.

"Hey, take it easy. I just want you to show them some little dance moves or steps, whatever you call it. They could pick it up. They're pretty sharp."

Some men from a construction crew dressed in dirty jeans and T-shirts sat at the table next to them. None of them seemed to care how loud their conversation or laughter was.

"Couldn't we talk about this some other place?"

"You're right." Trey stood up. "Let's talk about it later."

They left the restaurant and walked down the sidewalk in silence. Jenni wished her heart were not so troubled by this gentle man and the children he taught. Or was it her own feelings that troubled her? She wasn't even sure anymore.

"A penny for your thoughts," Trey said.

"And what would you do with them once you had them?" Jenni asked with only a hint of a smile.

"Put them in a box and treasure them." Trey put his arm

around her and pulled her to his side.

Jenni smiled, thinking to herself that he wouldn't treasure her thoughts and fears concerning the children. "I hate to run," she said, "but I've really got a lot to do."

"Would you just think about working with the kids?"

Jenni looked off in the distance. How could she explain her feelings and fears?

"Please!" Trey pleaded.

"Okay," she said reluctantly. "I'll think about it." But Jenni knew that no matter how much she thought, she would still come up with the same answer—she would not teach Trey's kids.

six

Beginning her cool-down exercises after a rigorous class regimen, Jenni placed her right leg on the *barre* and stretched her arms and body forward, then switched legs. She sat on the floor and rolled her feet between her hands, then put one leg in front, one in back, grabbed her front foot with her hands, and pulled her body forward to stretch the muscles.

"Jenni." Myra motioned to her from the doorway. Jenni pulled herself up from the floor and walked to the adjoining room, fanning her overheated face with her hands. She followed Myra into the empty lounge and dropped into a chair near the window.

"Have some orange juice." Myra handed her a small cardboard box of juice from the machine.

Jenni rubbed the cool box against her forehead, then popped the small straw into the container. "Thanks, Myra." Taking a long drink, she walked to the sink and swabbed her face and neck with wet paper towels. Finishing the juice, she pitched the box into the trash and went back to her chair by the window.

Myra stood beside her. "What's the problem, Jenni?"

"What do you mean?"

"I was in class with you this morning. You couldn't catch the combination. That's not at all like you."

"Guess everyone has an off day sometimes."

"Off day! What about that split *grand jeté*? You hardly got off the floor."

Jenni laughed. "That was really bad, wasn't it?" She patted her damp red cheeks with the wet towel.

"So what is it? Trey?"

"Yes and no."

"Meaning?"

"Yes, it concerns Trey, but no, it isn't Trey himself."

"Thanks for clearing that up."

"I'm sorry, Myra, but it's a little complicated." She leaned her head forward and placed the cool towel on the back of her neck.

"Look, Jenni, if you don't want to talk, fine. I'm just concerned about you."

Jenni got up from the chair, stretching her legs in the process. "It's not that I don't want to talk about it. It's just so. . ."

"So. . .what?"

Jenni turned to Myra. "Trey wants me to teach his kids to dance."

"That would be great, but when would you have time? Could you do it before class?"

"The time is the least of my worries."

"Then what is it? Working with kids would be fun, plus it would give you good experience for teaching classes later."

"Myra! They aren't just kids. They're. . .handicapped. Or disabled, as Trey calls them." Jenni paced in front of the window.

"Oh, that's right. I forgot. But that would be a challenge and you usually thrive on such things."

"I know. But this is different."

Myra walked in front of her, forcing her to look at her. "How is it different?"

"I'd rather not discuss it." Jenni walked to the sink and splashed her face with cold water once more, then patted it with a cloth towel. Draping the towel around her neck, she walked to the window and stared outside.

"You're in love with him, aren't you?"

Jenni whirled around to face Myra. "What are you talking about?"

"Trey Maddox. That's what I'm talking about."

"I'm not in love with Trey."

"Really?" Myra crossed her arms across her chest and

stood face-to-face with Jenni.

"I mean, I like him, but. . ."

"But what?"

"I've only known him for a month or so."

"And you can't fall in love in a month?"

Jenni paced the width of the room. "No. I don't know. You're right. I think I am in love with him. But nothing can ever come of it. We're so. . .different."

"If you're so different, why do you enjoy each other's company so much?"

"Well, not in that way. We like a lot of the same things, and we have fun together, but his work is his life."

"So is yours, Jenni."

"I know, I know. But those kids are almost a part of him. He talks about them all the time. He really, really loves them."

"And you can't?"

Jenni walked toward the doorway. "We'd better get back to rehearsal."

❧

At six o'clock Jenni decided to get ready for her date with Trey. John and Cindy had invited them to their home for dinner. Even though she looked forward to their company and an evening with Trey, she was less than excited over the idea of telling him she couldn't help with the children. She knew it wouldn't be easy for him to understand, but she must make him see that she was not a dance instructor and knew nothing about teaching children.

Brushing some blush across her cheeks, she stared at herself in the mirror. Whom was she kidding? She would say no to teaching those children even if she were a dance instructor. She knew that, and what was worse, after tonight Trey would know, too. He would also know that she could have no place in his life. The thought made her angry. *Why should he expect me to teach those kids anyway?* she thought to herself. Grabbing the mascara to touch up her lashes, she accidentally poked herself in the eye. "Ouch." She wiped her eye with a tissue then looked into the mirror. "Oh, great! Now I'll have to redo the whole thing."

Finishing her makeup, she again reprimanded herself for becoming involved with Trey. Hadn't she known all along that there could never be more than a summer romance between them? Why had she allowed herself to fall in love with someone who not only worked with disabled people but didn't even share her faith? Why had she even gone out with him? She usually made a habit of dating only Christian men. So what happened this time? Maybe it was the way Doug pushed her for a commitment. Of course she couldn't ignore the physical attraction she felt for Trey. But it was more than that. It was his gentle manner. The way he looked at her. The tenderness of his kisses. The way she felt when she was with him. The way he made her laugh. No one ever made her feel so alive and so loved.

"Oh, Papa, I wish you were here," she said aloud to the memory of her grandfather. "I know you would like Trey and could give me good advice."

Jenni walked to the window and watched for Trey's car, hoping he would be early, giving them a chance to talk before going to dinner. She paced the floor awhile then went to the bedroom to examine herself in the mirror one more time. Tonight was important. She wanted to look her best. The soft white pantsuit accented her Florida tan. Her dark hair fell loose around her face except for the side she pulled back with her gold comb—the comb Trey had knocked out of her hair on the plane.

Approving of what she saw, she went back to her place by the window to watch for Trey. The wait proved short, as she saw his Blazer pull into the parking space below her window. She watched him get out of the car and start up the stairs. He was wearing white slacks and a pale blue-and-white-striped sweater that she knew would match his eyes perfectly. This was not going to be easy. Taking a deep breath, she opened the door just as Trey was about to knock.

"Hey, look at you," Trey said with a smile.

"Yeah, we almost match," Jenni said, indicating their white clothes.

"Are you ready?"

"Trey, could we talk? Just for a minute?"

"Sure," he said, stepping inside.

"Well, you know, I told you I would think about your idea of my teaching the children to dance?" Jenni kept a short distance between her and Trey.

"I can't wait. The kids will love you, Jenni, and you'll like—"

"Trey, wait." She held up her hand. "I. . .I can't teach the children. I'm sorry."

Trey was silent for a moment. "Why?" he asked in a hushed tone and walked toward her. "Is it your schedule? What is it?"

Jenni tried not to look at him. Why was he doing this? "I just can't, that's all."

"Tell me the truth, Jenni—can't, or won't?" He took hold of her arm and gently pulled her to him. "I know that's your business, but I'd really like to know."

Jenni hadn't anticipated such a question, yet she should have known Trey would ask. She tried to find the courage to tell him the truth, to tell him she was afraid to even be around disabled people, but she couldn't stand the thought of his walking out of her life. Besides, how could she explain her feelings in a sensible way? Would she say, "I'm sorry, Trey, but I'm afraid of those kids"? No, that would never do. It didn't even make sense to her.

"I. . .I can't," she finally answered and lowered her gaze so she didn't have to look into his searching eyes. "I'm just not an instructor. I'm not qualified, and I really don't have the time."

"I'll work with you on your schedule, Jenni. Thirty minutes, or even less, is all I ask." He looked at her pleadingly. "Just once a week, and I don't care if you're qualified or not."

Trey put his arms around her waist and pulled her to him. "You dance from your heart and that's what's important. The kids are very sensitive to people and their feelings. They would pick up your natural rhythm and your love for the music and dance. I know they would."

"But, Trey." Jenni was trying so hard to say no, and Trey was making it so difficult. "You have to understand—"

"Look, I have an idea." He was still holding her so close all she could think about was the smell of his cologne and the warmth of his breath against her neck. "Could you meet me tomorrow morning, about eight-thirty?"

"I. . .guess so. Why?"

"That's when the kids have music class. If you could come to the school at that time, you could see for yourself how they love music."

"But, Trey, it's not that simple," she said, bringing her mind to attention. She saw the questioning look in his eyes. She would have to tell him now or do as he asked. She hesitated for only a moment. "Okay, I'll be there."

"Great! Now back to other business." He pulled her toward him again.

"I think we should go." Jenni smiled. "John should have those steaks on the grill by now."

Trey reluctantly agreed and Jenni picked up her purse and sweater on the way out the door, wondering how she was going to handle the morning.

seven

Driving slowly through the school zone and into the parking lot, Jenni chose a parking space near the front entrance. There were very few cars and no children outside playing. She wondered if they still had recess as they did when she was a little girl in school. How she had loved recess—everyone exploding out of the school doors onto the playground, running. That's what she felt like doing now—running. Jenni said a quick prayer, took a deep breath, and got out of the car, her heart already pounding.

She kept reminding herself this was just a children's music class. And even though she knew her fears were irrational, she couldn't seem to get her emotions under control. As she entered the building, a young woman about her age, dressed casually in jeans and a pullover shirt, greeted her.

"Hi, can I help you?"

"Yes, I'm looking for Trey Maddox," Jenni said with more confidence than she felt.

"He's in the speech room. All the way to the end of the hall, then to your left."

"Is there a room number?"

"No. Oh, and I should tell you that you actually go inside the physical therapy room and you'll see Trey's room to the left. Once you get inside the PT room, you can't miss it."

Jenni took a step toward the hallway then stopped. "Will there be children in the PT room? I wouldn't want to disturb the physical therapist or be a distraction," she quickly added.

"Oh, no, it's no bother. She won't even notice. The kids come and go a lot. We don't have a real rigid schedule during the summer. And I don't think Trey has anyone with him right now, but if he does he will be through soon. I would offer to call him, but the intercom isn't working."

"Oh, that's fine. I'm sure I can find him," Jenni said, trying to cover her nervousness. "I'll just walk down there, if that's okay."

"Sure, it's fine." The young woman smiled, seemingly unaware of Jenni's mounting anxiety.

Jenni took a few steps toward the hallway, hands cold and heart pounding.

"You did say down this hallway?" she turned and asked again, trying to calm herself.

"Right. To the end and on your left."

"Yes, of course. Thank you."

Jenni walked slowly down the tiled hallway, wishing she were somewhere else—anywhere else—except here. The smell of fresh paint mixed with the odor of chalk dust and wood shavings. "Guess everything gets a facelift in the summer," she said aloud, noticing the bright yellow walls. She tried to put her mind on something besides her anxiety.

Slowly, methodically, she continued down the hall. A row of small white fountains lined about four feet of the wall, and Jenni stopped to get a drink of water to cure her dry mouth. Stooping to catch the flow of water, she was startled when someone from behind took hold of her arm. She jumped and whirled around to see a slender boy, about twelve years old, standing before her.

"Hi," the boy said, holding onto Jenni's arm as his glasses slid down his nose.

Jenni coughed a bit, choking on the water in her mouth. "Hello," she finally managed to say as she pulled away from his touch. He walked toward her. Jenni's pulse raced.

"Who are you?" the boy asked. His words came out slowly, with effort, as saliva drooled down his chin.

Jenni looked around for an adult, wondering where the child had come from.

"Do I know you?" the boy persisted, wiping his chin with his hand and staring at her with weepy blue eyes, magnified by the thick lenses of his glasses.

"No. No, you don't know me." Jenni tried to smile and speak slowly and calmly. "I. . .I'm visiting."

"What's your name?" he asked, walking toward her with a limp.

Jenni backed up to the wall and scooted down the cool, smooth surface toward the doorway. The boy followed, reaching toward her.

"My name is Jenni," she said, again looking around for someone, anyone who could help her. At that moment a small woman with curly gray hair came out of a room from across the hall.

"Russell, you're supposed to be going to PT. Remember?" She walked over to the boy casually and smiled at Jenni.

"This is Jenni," he said, saliva spewing as he spoke. "I was *meeting* her," he said.

The woman's eyes crinkled with laugh lines as she smiled at him. She put her arm around Russell's shoulders. "Well, did you shake hands with Jenni and tell her your name the way we practiced in class today?"

Russell had a look of surprise and delight at the realization that he had left something off his "meeting." He clumsily grabbed Jenni's hand and shook it with his wet one. "I'm Russell," he said proudly. "You're Jenni."

The gray-haired woman laughed aloud. "Well, that's close enough," she said, pulling Russell away from Jenni. "Come on, now, let's get you to PT," she said with an easy smile as she guided Russell toward the PT room.

Russell walked through the doorway where Jenni had stationed herself, his limp more noticeable. Suddenly she realized that she had pressed her back firmly against the wall behind her as if someone had just held a gun to her head. She stepped away from the wall, trying to release the tension in her body, and brushed her damp hand on her pant leg.

She pulled back her shoulders and stood as straight as a soldier, trying to regain her composure. "I can do this," she told herself. "There is nothing to be afraid of. I'm being ridiculous. I'll walk calmly through the room and find Trey." But just as she touched the doorknob the door burst open and a tall, thin girl exploded out of the room with the gray-haired woman following.

"Tanya, wait," she called. Tanya turned and saw Jenni for the first time and stared at her silently.

The teacher took hold of Tanya's arm and led her to Jenni. "Tanya, this is Jenni," she said calmly.

"Hello, Tanya," Jenni said as she put out her hand, determined to do a better job this time.

Suddenly Tanya began to scream and wave her hands in the air. Jenni plastered herself against the wall once more.

"Tanya, stop that!" the teacher said firmly. But Tanya's screams drowned out her words. She turned to Jenni. "Sometimes new things upset her," she said matter-of-factly.

"I'm so sorry," Jenni said, her voice trembling and her heart pounding so hard she could feel it in her temples. "I didn't mean to upset her."

"Oh, you didn't do anything. She does the same thing with us sometimes. Tanya!" she called after the girl, who was walking down the hall with a lopsided gait, still screaming. "I'd better go."

"I'm sorry," Jenni repeated again.

"Don't worry about it," the teacher called back and smiled as if nothing unusual had happened.

Jenni continued to stand flat against the wall, almost paralyzed, eyes burning from tears trying to surface. Finally she willed herself to touch the doorknob, but her hand trembled and returned to her side. She could hear Russell's voice inside and Tanya's screams down the hall. If only Trey would walk out, maybe she could actually make it to the music class.

Finally she stepped away from the wall and ran her fingers through her hair, pushing the long dark tresses behind her ears. She took deep breaths, holding each for several seconds, biting the inside of her lower lip as she did so. Again she willed herself to enter the PT room. She closed her eyes for a moment, took one more deep breath, and then took hold of the doorknob. She stood motionless, unable to turn the knob.

"I can do this! I *will* do this!" she told herself, blinking back the tears and clenching her teeth together. She tightened her hold on the doorknob and turned it, but just as she opened the door, Russell saw her and started toward her.

Jenni closed the door quickly and hurried back up the hallway and out of the building. Once outside, she ran to the car and fumbled with the keys, trying to unlock the door. She looked back at the building nervously, as if she expected the boy to follow her outside. Finally the key turned in the lock and she collapsed into the front seat of the car, taking hold of the steering wheel with a firm grip to stop her hands from shaking. She rested her head against the top curve of the wheel.

"I can't do it, Lord. I just can *not* do it!" she said aloud as tears fell to her lap.

eight

The phone was ringing when Jenni walked into the apartment and she ran to answer it.

"Jenni, it's Myra. How did it go at school?"

"I didn't stay long. What did you need?" Jenni didn't want to talk about her trip to school.

"Michelle just went home sick and Mrs. Thatcher wondered if you could take her part along with yours."

"I think so. It's a lot like mine. I can stay late and work with her partner."

"Good. I'll tell Mrs. Thatcher. See you soon."

Jenni changed quickly, grabbed her things, and went to the theater. As expected, rehearsal lasted longer than usual with the extra part and gradually the unpleasant events of the morning slipped from her mind.

It was late when she returned home, and after soaking in a hot bath, she fell into bed, exhausted. Half-conscious, she thought of the call she intended to make to Trey, explaining the happenings at school. She decided to wait till morning.

As soon as she was showered and dressed she called Trey, but there was no answer. Jenni decided he was probably already at school and she could wait and tell him tonight. He always watched her Friday night performance, then they would go for a late night drive to the beach. It was a habit Jenni had quickly come to enjoy. Glancing at her watch, she quickly grabbed her things and rushed out the door. She wanted to rehearse most of the day, making sure she had everything perfect for tonight.

During lunch break Jenni saw Trey making his way through the people backstage. She went over to meet him, wondering what brought him there in the afternoon.

"I see you're feeling well," Trey said without his usual smile.

"Yes, why?"

"Where were you yesterday?"

"Why are you being so sarcastic?"

"I just want to know why you didn't show up at school."

"I really don't like your attitude, Trey."

"Oh? What is my attitude supposed to be? I waited for you yesterday morning then tried to call all afternoon. What do you expect?"

"You know I have rehearsal every afternoon."

"And you knew I was expecting you at school yesterday morning." Trey stared at her expectantly, waiting for an answer that she couldn't provide.

"I couldn't make it," she said, surprising herself at the untruth. She started to walk away, but Trey grabbed her and turned her to face him.

"Then why didn't you call?" His voice took on a softer quality but was still firm.

"I was busy. One of the girls got sick and I took her place."

Trey fixed his gaze on her. "I'm sure you could have managed five minutes for a phone call."

"Yes, I guess I could have," she said with a hint of sarcasm. "I just forgot."

"Forgot?" Trey raised his voice.

"Yes, forgot!" Jenni's voice also escalated and a couple of the dancers looked toward them. Jenni walked over to a side chair and Trey followed. "I told you I was busy. Besides, what difference does it make?" She grabbed a shirt from the chair and jerked it over her head. "So I missed the music class. What's the big deal?"

"The 'big deal' is that I promised the kids you would be there, and you didn't show. I even thought you could be sick, but no, I find out—"

"Find out what, Trey?" she interrupted. "That I decided not to come? Well, that's exactly what happened," she said, knowing she was not being truthful but deciding not to tell him of her experiences. She started to walk away, but he stepped in front of her.

"Didn't it matter to you that I was concerned, or that I promised those kids you would be there?"

"You have no right to make promises for me."

"No right? You told me you would come!"

"And I told you why I wasn't there."

"You forgot? That's an excuse, not a reason."

"Well, I didn't go, and I won't go, so why don't we just drop it!" Jenni said, trying to lower her voice as she noticed other people glancing toward them.

"Oh, believe me, I'll drop it, all right." Trey stood glaring at her, hands on his hips. He walked forward until he was close enough for Jenni to hear him take long, angry breaths. Finally he spoke quietly. "They don't need people like you around anyway."

"What do you mean, people like me?"

"I mean prejudiced people. We don't need you."

"Prejudiced? Why would you say that? You've seen the people I work with. How can you accuse me of being prejudiced?"

"I don't believe I saw a disabled person around, especially a mentally challenged person."

"Trey, you're being ridiculous." Jenni threw up her hands as if to dismiss the subject.

"No, Jenni, I'm being honest. You didn't come to school yesterday because you didn't want to be around children with special needs. Right?"

"Okay! I don't like being around handicapped people."

Trey stared at her for a long moment. "You talk about your faith in God and the talent He has given you. Well, maybe, just maybe, Jenni, God intended for you to use that talent to help people rather than just entertain." He wheeled around quickly and walked out.

Jenni stood motionless, stunned, as if she had been slapped in the face. "Trey, wait!" Jenni started after him. "It's not what you think." But Trey was already out the door.

❧

Unable to sleep, Jenni got up and fixed herself a cup of hot tea. She walked out on the veranda and watched the sunrise. *What's wrong with me?* she asked herself. *Were Trey's accusations correct?* She had never seen him so angry. In fact, she had never even seen herself quite so upset. Maybe they were just too different to be compatible. Perhaps this was God's way of showing her that she was in the wrong relationship.

She walked back into the apartment and sat alone. Myra would be gone the whole weekend, so she had no one to talk with. She thought back over the heated argument with Trey. Suddenly she became angry again. What right did he, of all people, have to question her motives or her faith in God? She was the only one who could know God's will for her life. Yet, deep in her heart, she knew that she didn't know at all what God wanted her to do with her life. But she was doing what she was trained to do. Hadn't God given her this talent? Trey's words came back to her, stinging her conscience. *Maybe, just maybe, Jenni, God intends for you to use your talent to help people rather than just entertain.*

"What does he know?" Jenni said aloud and jerked herself to her feet. She walked to the kitchen and scrubbed the little cup squeaky clean, letting her angry thoughts take over. She had worked hard to become the ballerina she was today. Countless dance classes, aching feet and legs, endless rehearsals. How could a speech pathologist know anything about that!

Her anger spilled out as she cleaned the apartment, clanging more dishes into the sink, throwing clothes and towels into the hamper, then jerking the vacuum from its closet home. She polished the furniture and woodwork, even dusted the pictures on the wall. Still unable to let go of her thoughts, she scrubbed the sinks, the shower, and tub, and mopped the floors.

Finally the tiny apartment was spotless. Nothing, not even a dish or plant, was out of place, yet her anger had subsided only a little. Jenni looked around, trying to find something else to do. "Maybe I should clean the kitchen cabinets," she said aloud. Opening the doors, she noted the orderly cabinets and changed her mind.

"I think I'm going crazy. I'm talking to myself, that proves it."

She showered and slipped into a long white terry robe, her thoughts still on Trey. *What's wrong with me?* she asked herself for the second time. She walked into her bedroom. *Maybe he's right.* The thought made her angry. Standing in the middle of the room, she screamed at the absent Trey. "Why should it matter to me what you think? Besides, what do you know of my walk with God?" She sat down on the edge of the bed. "What do I know about my walk with God?" she asked in a hushed tone. Tears began to sting her eyes and soon rolled down her cheeks. She lay back on her bed and began to sob. It was the first time she had allowed herself to really cry since her grandfather's death.

"Oh, Papa, Papa, I need you so much. I'm afraid and I don't even know what I'm afraid of. Why did you leave me? You were the only one who would answer my questions and now I have questions no one can answer." As Jenni cried, a memory from her childhood came to mind. She and her grandfather had gone to a little country cemetery to place flowers on her father's grave. Papa put flowers on another grave, and Jenni asked whose it was.

"It's your daddy's brother, Benjamin."

"Did I know him?" she asked, placing fresh flowers from her grandmother's garden on the grave.

"No, darlin'. Ben died before you were born." Jenni saw tears slide down his tanned, leathery cheeks.

"What happened to him?"

"Well, I don't rightly know. The doctor guessed it was his heart."

"Was Ben old?" Jenni thought only old people died with heart trouble.

"No, darlin', he wasn't old. Just fourteen. It was one of the hardest things I ever went through in my life," Papa said, staring at the grave covered with fresh flowers.

"Harder than when my daddy died?" she asked with the innocence that only a child could possess.

Papa looked off in the distance, his straw hat shading his eyes. "In a way, yes, it was. You see, Ben was. . .different than other kids. In fact, most kids teased and made fun of him. He couldn't talk real good, couldn't do all the things other kids did. But he could whistle like the birds. Could imitate any one of them." Papa smiled at the memory.

"Ben never hurt a person or a creature in his whole life. The most gentle soul I ever did see, and he could make me feel like a giant with his bear hugs and sparkly little eyes. You see, sweetheart," Papa knelt down on one knee and talked directly to her, "Ben had a different kind of love. About as close to God's love as you can get. And I guess that's what made him different."

"Then why didn't kids like him?" Jenni asked.

"They were afraid of him."

"Why? He wouldn't hurt them."

"People are afraid of things they don't understand, darlin'. And Ben was a mystery to most folks. Why, he would hug folks he didn't even know. Just loved people. And your daddy . . .oh, he loved your daddy, and Jeff always protected Ben. I know Ben's death was mighty hard on your daddy, too." Papa paused as he pulled some grass and weeds from around Ben's grave, then pursed his lips, shook his head, and continued.

"But your mama and daddy was already married by then and that seemed to help Jeff a lot. But me. . .when Ben died I felt like my heart was tore right out of me. I just can't tell you how much I hurt and missed that boy." Tears began to fall again and Papa wiped them away with the back of his callused hand.

"I got real mad at God, too," Papa said, pushing his tall lean frame to a standing position. "Told Him Ben never hurt nobody in his whole life and He had no right to take him."

"What did God say?" Jenni asked with curiosity.

"Nothin'. God don't argue with us, darlin'. He knew I was hurtin' real bad and understood why I was mad. He didn't stop lovin' me just 'cause I yelled at Him. But it took me awhile to forgive God for takin' my Ben. I got real bitter. Just ask your grandma. She remembers. In fact, God used her to bring me back to Him. You see, I made a vow I'd never speak to God again."

"You, Papa?" Jenni asked in amazement. "But you love God and talk to Him all the time."

"Oh, I know that now, darlin'. But I was hurtin' somethin' awful back then. Finally one night your grandma said, 'God never made no promises when He gave us Ben. Why, He didn't even have to give him to us in the first place. Would you rather never had him at all?' " Papa walked over to Jeff's grave and began clearing it of weeds also. Jenni trailed along, doing whatever Papa did.

"Well, that started me thinkin'. Couldn't imagine never havin' had my Ben. And I knew your grandma was right but didn't want to admit it." Jenni smiled a little at that, knowing Papa still didn't like to admit Grandma was right about anything.

"But it was like there was this big hole in my heart that I couldn't fill," Papa said, looking up at Jenni. "So I finally decided to talk to God one more time. Didn't try to bargain or none of that. Just told Him I couldn't go on with the pain and all about bein' mad at Him and how I was sorry for blamin' Him and not rememberin' to thank Him for Ben in the first place. I guess that's what God was waitin' on 'cause a deep peace came in my soul. Don't know how to explain it. Just knew things would be okay. I didn't stop hurtin', but I stopped hatin'."

"What about when Daddy died?"

"Well, I grieved awful bad over Jeff," Papa said, as he tenderly brushed leaves and grass from the headstone. "I loved your daddy as much as I loved Ben. But I learned from Ben's death how to find peace in the middle of my pain. And I knew Ben and Jeff was havin' a homecomin' party in heaven." Papa stood up and pulled a white handkerchief from his pocket. He took off his sweat-stained straw hat, wiped his damp eyes and forehead, blew his nose, and stuffed the rag into his back pocket. Then he laughed out loud.

"Yep, they're up there celebratin' and we're down here cryin'. Now that don't make much sense, does it?" He laughed again. "Come on, little girl, we gotta get back to livin'. Your grandma's gonna come lookin' for us if we don't get back soon. And you know what we'll have to answer to if we make supper late."

❧

The sunshine streamed through the window of Jenni's apartment as she lay quietly on her bed. Why had she remembered that scene with her grandfather? It had been so many years ago. What was wrong with Ben? No one had ever really talked about it. *Mom would know,* she thought to herself. Maybe she should ask her sometime. In fact, she would call her mother tonight. Suddenly Jenni sat straight up on the edge of the bed, curiosity and a sense of urgency overtaking her. "Why wait till tonight?" she said aloud and picked up the receiver of the phone.

nine

Jenni's fingers trembled slightly as she punched out her mother's phone number. She didn't know why, but she had an uneasy feeling about the question she was about to ask her mother.

The phone was ringing. . .three times, four. . .maybe she wasn't home. There was some relief in the thought. But just at that moment she heard the pick-up of the receiver and responded to the familiar voice.

"Mom?"

"Jenni! I was just thinking about you."

"Oh, Mom, you always say that."

"And it's always true. How are you, honey? How's work and when are you coming home?"

"Mom, wait! I'm fine. Work is fine. And I'm not coming home right away. You know that."

"Well, I had just hoped—"

"Mom." Jenni interrupted what she knew would be a plea to come back home. "I need to talk with you about something."

"What's wrong?"

"Nothing's wrong!" Jenni answered, wondering why mothers always suspect the worst. "I just. . .I just want to ask you a question."

"About what?"

"Well, I was thinking about Ben, and. . .well, I wondered if you knew, uh. . ." Jenni hesitated a moment. "Mom, what was wrong with him? Do you know?"

"Whom are you talking about, Jennifer?" Jenni knew she had struck a dark chord with her mother when she called her Jennifer.

"I'm talking about Daddy's brother, Benjamin. What

happened to him?" Jenni paced the short distance the cord on her bedroom phone would reach and twirled a strand of hair around her finger.

"Why on earth would you be wondering about Benjamin? And you know perfectly well what happened to him. He died."

"I know he died," Jenni said, sitting back down on the bed. "But what was wrong with him?"

"Well, I think it was his heart or something. You're not sick, are you, honey?"

"No, Mom, I'm fine. But I remember Papa saying he was. . . different. What did he mean?" Jenni began to fidget with the coiled phone cord, wondering why she couldn't ask her mother the direct question she wanted to ask.

"Jenni, I don't understand this sudden interest in Benjamin. Besides, your father and I were married only a short while when Benjamin died."

"But you knew him?"

"Yes, I knew him, but not well."

"Then tell me about him."

"There is nothing to tell. He died at a very early age and your father was heartbroken."

"What about you, Mom?" The question slipped out before Jenni even thought.

"What kind of question is that? I told you I hardly knew the boy. He was. . .retarded or something."

"What do you mean, retarded or something?" Jenni's heart began to pound and her mouth was dry. Why didn't her mother want to tell her about Ben and why did she find herself getting upset?

"Oh, for goodness' sake, Jenni, I—"

"Mom!" Jenni interrupted. "I have a right to know."

"All right. He was retarded!"

"Did he have Down syndrome?"

"I don't know! I just remember that his eyes had sort of a slant to them and he had poor speech."

"I remember Papa saying he loved everyone and never hurt a creature but that most people didn't like him. Why? Why didn't you like him?" Jenny's pulse raced and she was surprised to find herself getting angry at her mother's feelings and being defensive of Ben.

"He was different, Jenni. He liked to hug me and it bothered me. I didn't want him touching me."

"Did he hug Daddy?"

"Of course he hugged your daddy. Jeff was his brother. He was used to him." Her mother's voice softened. "Jeff adored him."

Jenni felt a pain deep inside at the sudden realization of her father's tender love for his brother. She wished he were with her, that he could put his arms around her and help her understand all the jumbled feelings she felt deep inside. She fought back tears.

"Mom, why didn't you and Daddy have more children? Why was I your only child?" she asked, trying to remain calm in spite of her thoughts.

Her mother hesitated. "I really don't think that is any of your business, Jenni."

"You were afraid, weren't you? Afraid you would have a child like Ben?"

"Yes, I was. I worried myself sick when I was pregnant with you and when you were perfect and so bright, I didn't want to take a chance on having another child."

Jenni was silent, trying to make sense of what her mother was saying. Something inside her wanted to scream, "What if I hadn't been perfect? Would you have loved me?" Tears welled up in Jenni's eyes; she quickly blinked them back.

"Jenni, what is wrong with you? I want to know," her mother demanded.

"Nothing. No. I don't know. It's just. . .all my life I wanted a brother or sister. I always thought if Daddy had lived longer that. . .well. . .you know. And now, to find out the real reason. . ." Jenni paused. She finally asked the question aloud.

"Mom, what about me? What if I hadn't been perfect?" Her voice quivered as the tears finally overflowed and ran down her cheeks.

"You're being ridiculous, Jenni. I don't know what started you on this, but you have no idea—"

"But Daddy loved Ben!" Jenni nearly shouted, barely hearing her mother's words. "You said so yourself. And Papa cried when he talked about his death. Why didn't you at least talk about him, tell me about him? And why didn't you give me the chance to love a brother or sister, no matter what they were like?" Hot, stinging tears ran down Jenni's cheeks, and she tried to wipe them away with her hand.

"Stop it, Jennifer! Stop it right now. I won't discuss this any further."

Jenni gained control of herself. She felt exhausted. "I'm sorry, Mom," she said quietly. "I didn't mean to upset you. I just needed to know. . . ," her voice trailed off.

"Jenni, tell me what is bothering you," her mother pleaded, obviously upset by the conversation.

"Nothing. I'm just tired. I've been pretty stressed at work this week—guess it's getting to me." Jenni felt the need to think, to be alone. She wanted to get off the phone.

"Maybe you should take some time off, come home for a while—"

"No, Mom. I'll be fine. I really have to go."

"Get some rest, honey. I worry about you."

"I know," Jenni said, trying to put a smile in her voice yet all the while knowing her mother would not be deceived. She hurriedly said her good-byes. "Bye, Mom. See you soon. I love you."

Jenni hung up the phone and allowed herself to fall back on the bed and stare at the ceiling while silent tears dropped onto the bedspread. "My uncle had Down syndrome!" she said aloud. "And my mother was afraid of him, just like I'm afraid of Trey's kids."

Her mind raced back over the years of her mother's constant

praise, telling Jenni over and over how smart and perfect she was. She had pushed her to excel at dance. *Was it for me or herself?* Jenni wondered. Other things started coming into her consciousness. She remembered how a conversation about Ben was cut short when she entered the room while she and her mother were visiting her grandparents. And thc countless times her mother had shielded her from a disabled person, never answering her questions. She would just smile and say it was "unfortunate" for that person.

Jenni began to understand her compulsive need to be perfect. She always thought it came from within herself. But now she realized that, unknowingly, her mother had instilled it in her, needing that assurance that there was nothing wrong with her daughter—physically or mentally.

But what did all this information really do for her? Where could she begin to unravel the thoughts, the fears, the misconceptions that were tangled up inside of her? She knew what her grandfather would do. He would pray. Jenni knelt beside her bed, not even knowing what she wanted to say, but positive the Holy Spirit would help her.

"Lord, I am so confused and mixed up right now. I know that my mother's fears were wrong. Yet I harbor those same fears in my heart. I try so hard to be perfect—for You, for Mother, even for me. But now I see that it is exactly that desire for perfection that is driving me away from You and away from Trey. Father, forgive me for feeling superior to others. Forgive my fears and give me a love for others and the same kind of joy I see in Trey. I know I am stubborn and immature at times, and I don't want to be this way. But I'm afraid, Lord. Please take away my fears and give me peace. In Jesus' name I pray. Amen."

Jenni got up, washed her face, changed clothes, combed her hair, and put on a little makeup to hide the red puffiness of her eyes. She knew what she must do. She glanced at her watch. She would have time if she hurried.

ten

Hoping to make some explanation about her visit to the school, Jenni drove out to the little beach house where Trey lived but found no one there. The Blazer was gone. Only the old white van with its rust spots sat in the driveway. She walked over to the van and ran her hand over the peeling paint, remembering her trip with Trey from the airport to Cocoa Beach. Even then they were prone to misunderstandings. She had thought Trey was married with eight children because he talked about taking his "kids" to the beach in the old van. She smiled at the memory.

Jenni walked back to her car and sat for a few minutes with the door open, hoping Trey might return soon. She needed to tell him that she really did go to the school, then explain what happened. She also needed to tell him about Benjamin and about her mother's fears as well as her own. She couldn't let their relationship end this way.

"Maybe he's at the school," she said, as if someone were listening. Trey had mentioned that he sometimes worked on files or paperwork on Saturdays. She closed the door to the car and drove through Cocoa Beach and out to the school west of town. But Trey's car was not to be seen. She sat in the parking lot, wondering what to do next. Finally she drove away from the school and down the main street of town. As she came to the church that she attended on Sundays, she decided to stop and see if the pastor was in. Maybe he could help her with this problem. She needed to talk with someone. She got out of the car and walked slowly up the steps of the steepled church. The big double doors to the brick building were unlocked and she stepped inside.

The still, quiet interior made her feel uneasy. Strange that she had never noticed that church services weren't really quiet at all. Not this kind of quiet. She could hear her own footsteps on the carpeted aisle as she walked toward the back of the church that led to the offices behind the sanctuary and found Pastor White's study. The door was closed, so she knocked gently.

"Come in," called a cheery voice from inside. Jenni entered timidly.

"Pastor White," she said, barely stepping inside the doorway. "I'm Jenni Lawson. I hope I'm not disturbing you."

"Not at all, Jenni," he said, taking off his reading glasses. "And I know who you are. You didn't have to introduce yourself, but I appreciate it anyway." He smiled as he stood up behind his large desk and motioned Jenni to a chair.

"I think it would be hard to remember the names of everyone in your congregation," she said as she sat down in the mauve armchair.

"Well, I have to work at it, I admit. But I use lots of little memory techniques." He sat down in the armchair across from Jenni. "Take your name, for instance. Gin and the law don't go together except in your name, Jenni Lawson. See what I mean? And yes, I realize your name actually starts with a J, not a G. But that's a little about how it works."

"That's interesting," she commented. Noticing the pastor's graying temples and laugh lines around his hazel eyes, she wondered if her own father would have looked much like this man had he lived.

"But I don't think you came here to talk about my memory techniques, did you?" Pastor White asked.

Jenni looked at him and smiled. "No, I didn't," she admitted, but she couldn't seem to go any further. She didn't know where to begin and wondered if she should even be here as she traced the design of the fabric on the armchair with her finger.

"Why don't we talk about you," Pastor White suggested. "If I remember correctly, you are a fine ballet dancer. Am I right?"

"I try to be," Jenni said, wishing she felt more comfortable. She looked around the room at the cream-colored walls covered with pictures and certificates and blue miniblinds at the windows, thinking that the room didn't look masculine at all. A framed picture of the pastor's family sat on the desk.

"Jenni," Pastor White said patiently, "you don't have to tell me anything you don't want to, but I'm a good listener, if you need someone."

She bit her lower lip, looking down at the floor for a moment. "For some reason it's very hard for me to talk," she said, looking across at the pastor.

"I understand. I have a daughter just about your age, I would guess. And it's sometimes hard for her to talk with me, too. She thinks the world has changed so much that a fifty-year-old preacher wouldn't understand."

Jenni laughed a little, releasing some of her tension. "I feel kind of ridiculous. But I do need to talk with someone. My father died when I was four, so I always went to my grandfather with my problems, and now that he's gone I don't really have anyone to advise me." She hesitated, then continued. "I have a friend who thinks I should use my dancing to help people. He works with developmentally disabled children and wants me to teach them to dance. I want to do what God wants me to do, but. . ." Jenni paused. "Would God ask me to do something that. . .well. . .seems impossible for me to do?"

Pastor White sat silently, watching Jenni as she talked. She hurried on, wondering if there was any coherency to what she was saying.

"I know I'm not explaining this very well. Trey, the person I'm talking about, is. . .special to me, so I tried to do what he asked. I even went to the school where he works, but I got scared and left. Trey doesn't know I was there and now he thinks I broke my promise and that I'm prejudiced. And I think maybe he's right, that I really am prejudiced." Jenni's voice quivered as she fought back tears. "I'm probably not making any sense at all, am I?"

Pastor White leaned forward slightly in his chair. "Am I understanding that you are afraid of the children Trey teaches?"

"Yes. Isn't that silly?"

"No. Many people have irrational fears. In fact, most of us do at some point in our lives."

"But Trey doesn't understand!"

"Have you tried to talk with him about your fears?"

"No. I don't know how. And he is so mad at me right now, I can't talk with him. And what's worse is that I profess to be a Christian, and look what kind of witness I've been to him."

"I see. So you think you have ruined your Christian witness to Trey because of your fears?"

"Yes. And my actions. I wanted to explain, but when he got so angry, so did I, and now I don't know what to do."

"Jenni, are you in love with Trey?"

"Yes."

"Do you love him enough to go to him and explain what you just told me?"

"I don't know. I think so. I drove to his house this morning, but he wasn't there."

"Why don't you try again?"

"But what if he doesn't understand?" She looked at the pastor with pleading eyes.

"That's the chance you have to take. But I think he will, and I think he could be the key to helping you overcome your fears. You don't want to be afraid of people with disabilities, do you, Jenni?"

"No, of course not. But I just can't seem to get past it." Jenni felt tears trying to surface and quickly blinked them back.

"Then talk to Trey. Let him help you. God doesn't want you to fear people. The Bible tells us that. He doesn't want you to be anxious or upset." He waited briefly for a response, then continued. "People with disabilities are just like you and me, Jenni. They have the same feelings and emotions. They have hopes and dreams and people like Trey help make those dreams come true."

"I know you're right but. . . ," her voice trailed off.

"Still a little scary?"

Jenni nodded.

"I understand. That's why I think you should talk to Trey. Sometimes God uses other people to help us. Maybe God really does want you to teach those children."

"I don't see how I could possibly do that."

"If God wants you to work with developmentally disabled children, rest assured He will give you the strength and the desire to do so."

Jenni lowered her gaze as tears slipped down her cheeks.

"Let God use you, Jenni. You are wonderfully gifted and have such a loving, sensitive spirit. I believe God has great things planned for you, but you must be willing to step out in faith."

Jenni dabbed at her eyes with a tissue.

"I hope I haven't sounded too much like a parent," Pastor White said with a smile. "Remember, I told you I had a daughter about your age."

Jenni stood up to leave. "Thanks for your help." Pastor White stood and walked to the door with her.

"I'll be praying for you, Jenni. I'm confident that God will show you what to do. And don't think for a moment that you have lost your Christian witness."

"Thank you," Jenni said with a smile. After she got into the car and started toward her apartment, she decided to swing back by Trey's house one more time. The Blazer was in the driveway. She walked to the door and stood for a moment, then knocked. There was no answer. Her anxiety mounted and she felt the urge to leave but fought against it as she knocked again, this time a little harder to be sure she was heard. Still no answer. She walked around to the back and looked off toward the ocean. A short distance away she saw Trey walking along the beach, stopping occasionally to look out over the water then run his fingers through his sun-bleached hair, something she had seen him do dozens of times.

She thought about calling out to him but decided to walk down to the beach to meet him. She wanted to talk with him face-to-face, tell him what had happened and see understanding in his blue eyes. Suddenly she stopped short. What if that wasn't what she saw? Pastor White could be wrong. What if he didn't understand her fears? She looked out at Trey again, then turned and walked back to her car.

❧

After slipping into her costume, Jenni checked her makeup and hair. Her solo was next. Nervousness and excitement mingled inside her. When she was onstage during her *pas de deux*, she saw Trey in the audience—second row, aisle seat, where he normally sat on Friday nights. She wondered why he was here and if the woman beside him was his guest.

It had been a week since their argument. He hadn't called and she often found herself thinking about his blue eyes, the scent of his cologne, even his perfectly even white teeth that gleamed against his bronzed complexion. Many times she reprimanded herself for not telling Trey the truth about why she wouldn't teach the children, or why she even allowed herself to get involved with him in the first place. Hadn't she known from the beginning that their lives were very different? She had decided it was time to accept that fact and remember why she was in Florida. But she hadn't counted on Trey's showing up at her performance. Now what was she supposed to do?

Jenni paced a little offstage as she watched for her cue. "Concentrate, concentrate," she said aloud to herself. "Just don't look at him. Focus your attention on the dance." The director motioned to Jenni. She lifted her head high, straightened her back, and squared her shoulders. The violins in the orchestra began the love song, and Jenni made her entrance.

Her heart listened to the sweet sounds of love while her mind told her body what to do. She was in tune with the music, with the love and emotions it brought forth. Her body moved gracefully, giving the music words and emotions too deep to speak. It was as though she were dancing of a love lost, rather than one shared, and she put every ounce of her energy into the dance, then ended with a *révérence*.

The audience came to their feet, clapping wildly. Jenni bowed, then left the stage, but the applause continued. Happily, Jenni returned to the stage for the curtain call—but she had to force herself to keep smiling as she looked out over the audience. The seat in the second row was empty.

eleven

"Please come with us, Jenni," Myra pleaded. "Everybody is going out for dinner and you need to have some fun."

"I'm just not in the mood," Jenni said.

"You worked so hard on that solo and tonight's performance was absolutely perfect. Let's celebrate!"

"Myra, I just don't feel like celebrating. You go and I'll see you at the apartment later. Then you can tell me how much fun I missed." Myra gave her an agitated look and walked away. Jenni changed clothes quickly, removed her stage makeup, and walked out the back door of the theater.

She couldn't help but think how different the evenings in Cocoa Beach were from the hot, sticky nights in Oklahoma. She especially liked the beach at night with the cool breeze blowing across the ocean. Leaving Florida would be hard and the summer was passing quickly. All too soon she would be on her way back to the dance company in Oklahoma.

As she walked toward the car, a movement startled her. She turned quickly and saw Trey. Her heart started pounding.

"I hope I didn't scare you," he said, stepping in front of her.

"A little," she said, her pulse still racing.

"Jenni, could we talk?"

For a full week Jenni had chided herself about not making explanations to Trey. Now here was her opportunity and she didn't think she was ready. More than anything she wanted to be with him, to have him hold her in his arms as he had done so many times. But another part of her wanted to walk away. Perhaps it would diminish the pain of leaving when the summer ended.

"I don't think we have much to say," she finally answered.

"Maybe you don't, but I do. Could we go for a drive?

To the beach, maybe?"

Jenni was silent for a moment. Where could this possibly lead? Only to more trouble and more pain. Their lives could never fit together.

"I don't think so, Trey. I'm really very tired." She started toward the car, but Trey took hold of her arm and turned her to face him.

"Please. I have to talk to you."

She hesitated, knowing she should get in her car and go straight home, but somehow she found herself giving in to his plea, thinking perhaps she should make an attempt at an explanation. At least their relationship could end on a better note.

"Okay, but only for a little while."

On the short drive to the beach, Trey praised her performance. "You always amaze me, Jenni. You share your heart and soul when you dance."

That was what she was afraid of. They came to a sandy beach and got out of the car. Trey slipped Jenni's sweater over her shoulders. She shivered a little, more from his touch than the cool ocean air. Jenni took off her shoes as they began to walk along the sandy shore, letting the water ripple over her ankles.

"Jenni, I know you probably can't forgive me for the way I acted last week, but I want to say that I'm sorry. I don't know what happened to me. I've thought about it over and over and still can't believe I said those things." Trey stopped walking and turned Jenni toward him. "Please believe me. I'm really sorry. I have a terrible temper. I admit it. I was totally out of control and should have apologized sooner, but I was afraid you wouldn't want to see me."

She pulled away gently, not trusting her emotions. They walked a little farther. She could see the white caps of the waves in the bright moonlight and feel the cool ocean breeze against her face.

"Trey, I'd like to explain what happened that day."

"You have nothing to explain."

"Yes, I do. You said I was prejudiced."

"I'm sorry. I—"

"No, let me finish. I thought about it a lot. I think you're right."

"Jenni—"

"Wait till I'm through, please." She tried to choose her words carefully. "Trey, I'm not sure how to say this, except that I'm afraid. That's why I didn't come to your class."

"I don't understand. What could you be afraid of?"

"I don't know. I just know that when I was out in that hall alone with Russell and then when Tanya started screaming, I got scared and left."

Trey stopped abruptly. "You mean you actually came to the school?"

"Yes." Jenni turned to face him and the confusion she saw in his eyes. "I even got to the PT room. And I tried. I really, really tried to go in, but I. . .I was. . .so scared. I'm sorry." Tears ran down her cheeks. Trey cupped her face in his hands and wiped her tears away.

"Jenni, what is it? Tell me."

"I've thought about it over and over and. . .I guess I really am prejudiced."

"Sweetheart, don't say that." Trey pulled her to him, holding her tightly.

"But it's true." Her voice was barely audible. "Why else would I act that way?"

Trey held Jenni out from him and took hold of her chin, tilting her head up. Even in the moonlight, Jenni could see the concern on his face. "Sweetheart, you've got to tell me what this is about. I don't understand."

Jenni looked directly into his eyes. "I'm terrified. I thought it was the children that frightened me. But I finally figured out that it's not really the children at all. It's me!" By now she was shaking as tears spilled out in sobs. Trey caught hold of her shoulders.

"Tell me what you're talking about, Jenni. You, afraid? Of what?"

"Of not being perfect, not being in control. Not being a good Christian. Oh, I don't know." Jenni buried her face in Trey's chest and cried, "I'm just scared and I've never felt this way before."

Trey circled his arms around her, then led her over to a boardwalk from one of the hotels. They sat down together.

"Now start at the beginning. Tell me what happened to make you feel this way."

"Well, at first I didn't know what was wrong and didn't really care." She took the handkerchief Trey offered. "But then I decided I wanted to know why I felt the way I did." She told him about Benjamin, and her mother's fears, and how she began to unravel the puzzle to her own irrational fear of the disabled.

"But I can't conquer it. That day at school proved it. I don't know what to do." Jenni turned her head away, wishing the tears would stop.

"Why didn't you tell me this before?"

"I was afraid you wouldn't understand."

"Oh, Jenni." He looked out toward the water, and the silence was broken only by the sound of the waves hitting the shore. He looked back at her. "I'm sorry I pushed you to come to the school. That wasn't fair."

"You didn't know. You love those kids. I know you only wanted to share that. I just didn't know how to handle it. I even talked with Pastor White, but I still haven't handled things well."

"Sweetheart, I think you've handled things beautifully," Trey said, holding her in his arms and stroking her hair. "I'm just so sorry I hurt you. I hope you can forgive me and we can start again."

"You mean you want to, knowing about my fears?" Jenni looked into his eyes.

"More than ever."

She nodded her agreement as she snuggled into his arms. But this time she would handle things differently. She would pray and let God be in control, and if He decided her relationship with Trey was to end with the summer, then she would accept that.

twelve

After changing from leotard and tights into her bathing suit, Jenni walked into the living room, where Myra was relaxing on the sofa, feet propped on the coffee table.

"Sure you won't change your mind and go swimming?"

"No. I think you and Prince Charming can do without me."

"Myra, I told you that Trey invited both of us."

"Oh, I'm teasing. But I really don't want to go. I'm exhausted. Where do you get the energy to swim after rehearsal?"

"I'm tired, too. But the water sounds refreshing. Besides, Trey said the place is really pretty. I may just lie beside the pool and take in the scenery."

"Well, please do it without me. I may still be in this spot when you get back." Myra laughed. "I'm glad you're happy again, Jenni. I was getting worried about you. Everything going okay with you and Trey now?"

"Hmm, I hope so."

"Do I detect a note of reluctance?"

"Guess I'll know more tonight. I'm going to ask Trey to go to church with me. He doesn't like to discuss religion, so we'll see how this goes."

"Good luck."

"Thanks." Jenni grabbed her purse and keys. "Say, why don't I pick up some Chinese food on my way home? We'll splurge tonight."

"Oh, Jenni, would you? Maybe I'll be more energetic by then." They both laughed. "Do you suppose I'd have as much energy as you have if I fell madly in love with some handsome guy?"

"Rest, Myra. Rehearsal seems to be getting to you." Jenni

started out the door.

"Oh, wait. I almost forgot." Myra picked up a letter from the coffee table and waved it in the air.

Jenni winced. "Doug?"

"You guessed it. When are you going to tell him about Trey?"

Jenni groaned. "Soon."

Myra raised questioning eyebrows.

"I just don't know what to tell him—and don't look at me that way. I'll tell him about Trey before I go home. Is that good enough?" She hurried out the door before Myra could answer.

The Kalua sat right on the beach, surrounded by palms and more tropical flowers and foliage than Jenni had ever seen in one place. Trailing purple bougainvillea, hot pink hibiscus, and banana palms filled the courtyard surrounding the pool.

Trey waved and Jenni walked over and sat on the edge of the pool. "This is beautiful, but are you sure it's okay for us to be here? Isn't this a hotel or something?"

"It's both hotel and apartment complexes. And it's okay to be here. I know the manager."

"Lucky you."

"I lived in one of the apartments for a while when I first moved to Cocoa Beach. That was before he built that big deck and the boardwalk to the beach." He motioned toward the ocean, then looked beyond Jenni toward one of the chaises. "Chrissy, do you want to put on your bathing suit and come in the water?"

Jenni looked around and saw the dark-haired, dark-eyed little girl shake her head no.

"You didn't tell me you were bringing Chrissy."

"I didn't know. Her foster mother had a little emergency with one of the other children and couldn't get to the school, so I told her I'd take Chrissy with me. She should be picking her up soon."

"Always the good guy." Jenni hated the way she was acting.

She should be able to interact with a child, but she just didn't know how to talk with a child who couldn't talk back. Chrissy sat down on the side of the pool beside Jenni and smiled at her.

"Hi, Chrissy," Jenni said, her heart already beginning to race. She had no idea what else to say or do.

Trey stood in the water in front of the two. "Chrissy, do you remember seeing Jenni at Disney World?"

She nodded in agreement, then started waving. Jenni followed her gaze to the courtyard gate and saw her foster mother. Chrissy jumped up, then suddenly grabbed Jenni around the neck and hugged her. Jenni's heart began to pound, but the child was gone before she had a chance to think about a proper response.

"She likes you," Trey said.

"She doesn't even know me." Trey didn't respond to the comment. Feeling guilty over her abrupt response, she asked, "Will she ever speak?"

"I don't know. I certainly hope so. Hey, are you going to get wet or just sit there and look beautiful?"

"Well, since you put it that way, I think I'll just sit here."

"Oh, no, you're not." Trey swam over and grabbed her foot and began to pull.

"Trey, don't!"

He laughed and grabbed her around the waist and pulled her into the pool, dunking her under the water.

Jenni screamed before she hit the water, then came up coughing and gasping for air. She gripped the edge of the pool and crawled out of the water, hands shaking as she pushed wet hair from her face.

Trey swam over to the side, the smile gone from his face. "Are you okay? You're shaking. What's wrong?" His voice was steady, but Jenni could hear the concern in it.

"I can't swim."

"Oh, no! I don't believe it. Didn't you take lessons as a kid?"

She shook her head. "Huh-uh. Always had ballet classes."

"Well, little ballerina, it's time you learned to swim." He took hold of her hands.

"Trey, please don't pull me in!"

"I'm not. I'm going to help you learn to swim. Now ease into the water."

"I don't want to." She jerked her hands away.

"Jenni, you shouldn't live around this much water and not know how to swim. It's dangerous. Now get in the water."

She hesitated.

"Please!"

"Oh, okay, but I'll be a very poor student."

"You've already proven that."

"Thanks!"

An hour later Jenni could actually float on her back and stomach and even paddle around a little without her feet touching the bottom of the pool. She climbed out of the water and grabbed a towel. "I've got to go home."

Trey took a towel and brushed it over his blond hair. "You did great."

"I wasn't such a poor student after all, huh?"

"Actually, I think it was the superior teaching."

She reached over and hit him with her towel. "If the teacher doesn't watch it, he will end up back in the pool at the hand of his student."

Trey laughed. "Come on, I'll walk you to your car."

"Good. I have something I want to ask you."

"What is it?"

They walked along the shaded path. "I want you to go someplace with me."

"Sure. Where do you want to go?"

"I want you to go to church with me on Sunday."

He stopped abruptly and stared at her.

"Trey, please."

"You know I don't want to go to church."

"But I want you to go. Doesn't that mean anything?"

He tilted his head up and ran his fingers through his hair.

"If I say no, are you going to keep asking?"

She nodded in agreement.

"That's what I thought."

"Why won't you go? What are you afraid of?"

"I'm not afraid of anything. I just don't want to go. No! The answer is no."

Jenni walked on toward the car silently.

"You mean you're not going to challenge that?"

"No."

Trey beamed. "Good."

Jenni opened the car door. "Thanks for the swimming lesson."

"One isn't enough. You give me a time when you can make it next week, and we'll work some more. Glenn doesn't mind our coming at all. He even likes for me to bring the kids once a week for swimming and a picnic on the deck. They love it here."

"I don't think I want any more lessons." Jenni smiled at Trey.

He cocked his head to one side and looked down into her face. "You are going to learn to swim, aren't you?"

"No."

"You're not that scared of the water, are you?"

"No. I'm not afraid of anything. I just don't want to do it," Jenni said, mimicking Trey.

"I can't believe you're doing this."

She put her towel on the car seat and sat down and started to close the car door, but Trey held it open, glaring at her.

"Okay! What time do I pick you up on Sunday?"

thirteen

Jenni rushed through a shower and put on a pale yellow suit with a long straight skirt and matching jacket. She gathered her dark hair at the nape of her neck, secured it with a mother-of-pearl hair clip, and then examined herself in the mirror. No, the earrings and necklace weren't right. She quickly changed the jewelry and was trying to clasp the necklace when she heard a knock at the door. Naturally, Trey would be early when she was running late. He knocked again.

"I'm coming." She rushed to open the door and caught her breath at the sight of him in a gray suit and coordinating tie. She was accustomed to seeing him in shorts or jeans and sweaters, even a sports coat, but this morning she couldn't take her eyes off him. Trey caught her look of amazement as he stepped into the apartment.

"I'm not completely uncivilized, Jenni. I do know how to dress for church."

"Why, you look. . .gorgeous!"

"That's not exactly the word I was hoping to hear, but I'll accept it as a compliment. And you, my sweet, look absolutely beautiful—or should I say handsome, since I'm gorgeous."

"Well, thank you, but I need your help. Here." She handed the necklace to Trey. "I can't seem to get the clasp to work." She held her hair off her neck and turned her back to him. Trey slipped the chain around her neck.

"Good grief, it's so tiny I can hardly keep hold of it. Now, I think I got it."

Jenni started to move away, but Trey circled his arms around her. "Trey, we need to leave for church." She turned around to face him.

"Couldn't we skip church and just go on to the beach?" She

could see the fun dancing in his eyes.

"Trey Maddox, you promised you would go to church with me this morning."

"I know. I know. But don't forget, we bicycle to the beach afterwards."

"I have picnic food in the refrigerator. Now let's go."

They seated themselves on a pew about halfway down the sanctuary. Trey rolled the church bulletin in his hand and tapped it against his leg. Jenni noticed and smiled at him. "Why are you so nervous? It's just a church service."

"I'm not nervous, just—"

"Good morning, Jenni. Glad to see you."

"Hello, Pastor White. I'd like you to meet a friend of mine, Trey Maddox."

The pastor extended his hand for a handshake. "Trey, glad to have you. Hope you enjoy the service and visit us again."

"Thank you," Trey said. The pastor walked away, greeting more people and shaking hands with everyone he met.

Trey pulled at his tie uncomfortably and frowned at Jenni. She smiled and shook her head at his discomfort. He took her hand in his. "Maybe I'll survive if you hold my hand."

"Now that's a new one. I don't think I've ever heard that line before."

Trey gave a broad smile. "Thought it was worth a try."

The choir filed in to organ music, then began a medley of old hymns, ending with "Rock of Ages." The choir director turned to the congregation. "Please stand and turn in your hymnals to page 165, 'Amazing Grace, How Sweet the Sound.' "

Jenni held the book between them, and Trey sang out clearly in his baritone voice, never looking at the words. When they sat down, she whispered, "I thought you didn't go to church."

"Everyone knows 'Amazing Grace,' " he whispered back, then turned his attention to the front of the church.

The pastor stood in front of the podium. "Today we're

going to talk about God's faithfulness in hard times, and we're going to be looking at a book in the Bible that we seldom read. If you will turn to Habakkuk 3:19. . ."

The church bulletin slid off Jenni's lap and she put her Bible beside her as she leaned down to retrieve the bulletin from the floor. Trey picked up the Bible, turned to the Scripture, and held it between them while the pastor read the text, but Jenni hardly heard a word. She kept wondering how Trey found the Scripture with such ease. Even she couldn't remember where the book of Habakkuk was located except that it was somewhere in the Old Testament.

"The book of Psalms also has a lot to say about God's faithfulness," the pastor continued. Trey turned to Psalm 18, as the pastor requested, not seeming to notice Jenni's look of surprise. He seemed completely at ease using the Bible. She wondered about it but decided it was probably best not to mention it.

Getting into the car after the service, Trey commented, "You know, we could have walked this distance from your apartment. What is it, half a dozen blocks?"

"Have you ever tried to walk six blocks in high heels, especially with sore feet?"

Trey smiled. "Guess that's why we drove the car. You sure you can handle the bicycle ride?"

"That shouldn't be a problem. I'll have on sneakers and socks."

❧

Trey sped ahead on his bike, trying to get Jenni to race, but she was enjoying the leisurely ride. The ocean was right off the highway and palm trees waved in the breeze. She felt a freedom with the wind cooling her face and blowing her hair, now pulled up in a ponytail. Trey motioned toward a strip of sandy beach with trees for shade and pulled over. He had the picnic basket off his bicycle and was spreading a cloth on the sand when Jenni pulled up.

Somehow the scene made her realize the gentleness that

Trey possessed. It was like seeing him with one of the children. She had read in the Bible about a "gentle spirit" but somehow had always equated it with mothers and grandmothers, even though her grandfather was a perfect example. Now she knew that she could never marry a man without this quality.

"How do you feel?" He walked over and unstrapped the cooler of soft drinks from Jenni's bike.

"Great. Just a little warm and thirsty."

"It will be cooler on the ride back."

"Oh, I'm fine." She patted her flushed cheeks with cool water and brushed away the wet hair sticking to her face.

Trey placed a quick kiss on her damp forehead. "I don't know about you, but I'm starved."

"No argument here."

After sandwiches and fruit, they stretched out on a beach towel.

"Someday we're going to do that," Trey said, propping himself up on one elbow.

"Do what?" She followed his gaze to a sailboat on the water.

"Just the two of us, sailing into the sunset," he said dramatically.

"Well, you'd better change oceans, since the sun rises on this one."

"So. . .we'll sail the other ocean."

Jenni smiled but didn't answer. Someday was too far away and the present was looming in front of her, and that meant eventually walking away from Trey at the end of the summer. But she didn't want to think of that right now.

Jenni propped herself up to face Trey, her head resting against her hand. "Why did you stay?"

"You mean why did I stay in Florida?"

Jenni nodded.

"Lots of things," he said, looking pensive. "I liked the people, the beach, the weather, and, of course, the job."

"You really enjoy working with kids, don't you?"

"Yes, I do."

Jenni sensed a reluctance on Trey's part to discuss his work because of her reaction to the children. She knew he didn't want to upset her.

"Tell me how you got into this type of work," Jenni urged.

"Oh, it's a long story and I don't want to bore you."

"You won't bore me. I want to know."

"You sure?" Trey asked with the smile Jenni loved so much.

"Yes. Tell me."

Trey sat up straight.

"When I was in college, my sister was involved in a. . .serious car accident. Besides broken bones and internal injuries, she also suffered partial paralysis and loss of speech. I visited her at the hospital every day and watched her struggle to answer a question. It was frustrating, and I hated the fact that I wasn't able to help her." He hesitated, then added, "I also hated God for doing that to Katie."

"Trey, God didn't do that to your sister," Jenni quickly interjected. Trey was silent. "I'm sorry," she said. "I interrupted. Tell me what happened."

He picked up a stick from the ground and drew circles in the sand while he spoke. "Well, I was there one day when a speech pathologist came to work with her. I asked her if there really was any hope that Katie could talk again. She gave me a whole new perspective and I became determined to help Katie speak. I worked with her every day, even some nights. Pushed her too hard, in fact." Trey paused and looked out at the water, the sun reflecting in his blue eyes.

"Not many people would do that," Jenni said.

"It wasn't a difficult decision." Trey looked down at the sand but didn't continue.

"So. . .did she learn to talk again?"

"Yeah, she did," he said flatly, seeming to reflect on something. "At first I wanted immediate results, to have words come from her after three days or a week." Trey smiled.

"That's when I learned patience. Nothing ever comes easy. But after some weeks Katie was able to talk a little. At least she could answer yes and no and ask for what she wanted. Something most people thought she would never be able to do again. I guess you could say I felt proud, although it was deeper than that. But it was a feeling I never lost. So. . .I changed my major in school and studied to be a speech pathologist."

As they sat quietly for a moment, Jenni thought about his words. When had she allowed God to use her to help someone or make someone's life better? Suddenly her own faith seemed superficial. She wanted all the good without the bad. Oh, she hadn't minded the hard work and long hours required for her dance, but was she willing to use this talent, this gift from God, to help someone else? It was the same question Trey had asked her after their argument about the children.

"I told you I would bore you," he said, scooping sand on Jenni.

"You haven't bored me at all," she said, brushing the sand away. "Sounds like a miracle to me."

Trey said nothing.

"You know, sometimes God uses us to help with His miracles," Jenni said.

"Well, I just don't happen to believe in miracles, or God either, for that matter."

Jenni bolted upright from the towel and positioned herself face-to-face with him. "Trey! How can you say that?"

"Because that's how I believe, and don't preach to me, Jenni."

"I'm not going to preach to you. I just want to know why you believe—"

"Don't you mean why I *don't* believe?" He let out a low chuckle.

"That's not funny. What about your sister? Don't you think God had something to do with her recovery?"

"No, I don't!"

"I can't believe you would say that. God loves all of us. He wants the best for our lives. And He used you and others to help your sister speak and recover."

"She died!" Trey threw the stick on the ground and stood up, turning his back to Jenni as he looked out over the water.

She sat still for a moment, the shock of his words ringing in her ears. *No wonder he's so bitter.* She got up and walked over to Trey, putting her hand on his arm. "I'm. . .sorry, Trey. I don't know what to say. But you can't blame God."

Trey whirled around. "Then whom would you suggest, Jenni?" His eyes flashed with anger. "She was just a kid! She never got to know what it was like to be a cheerleader or to go to a senior prom, or even drive a car."

Jenni caught her lower lip between her teeth and fought back tears. She wanted to comfort him in some way but didn't know how.

"And you know something else?" Trey was standing in front of her, his jaw taut, his eyes filled with pain. "A lot of the kids I work with will never get to do any of those things either. Now, do you want to tell me why your loving God would allow that?"

Shocked at the anger spilling out of Trey, she could only stand and stare. She had no answers. Finally she took hold of his arm. "Trey, I'm—"

He pulled away from her. "I don't want to talk about it anymore, Jenni." He tilted his head upward toward the clouds gathering overhead. "We've got to get out of here or we're going to get drenched on the way back."

They gathered the picnic leftovers in silence and rode back to Trey's house, barely beating the afternoon downpour.

fourteen

"What are you doing?" Myra surprised Jenni as she rummaged through the cabinet under the kitchen sink.

"Looking for the laundry detergent."

"It's behind the dishwashing liquid. But I thought you were spending the day with Trey."

"I did. Most of it anyway. The thunderstorm finished the picnic." She reached under the cabinet and retrieved the box of detergent before turning to Myra. "We were having a friendly disagreement anyway."

"Hm-mm. Must not have been too friendly or you wouldn't be home doing laundry."

Jenni ignored Myra's comment and pitched the detergent into the laundry basket. "Got anything you want me to wash?" She picked up the basket of clothes.

"Just towels and washcloths." Myra started toward the bathroom.

"I've got them," Jenni called after her. "Oh, my book." She dropped the basket and ran to the bedroom, returning with a paperback. "Thought I'd do a little reading *while the washer turns,*" she said dramatically.

Myra laughed. "Good luck. But look out for Mrs. Pollard. She watches that laundry room like a hawk."

"Yeah, I've noticed." Jenni picked up the basket and started toward the door. "Guess I'd be the same way if I owned an apartment complex. Probably afraid someone will destroy one of the appliances."

"Don't kid yourself. It's not the appliances she's interested in. It's the people."

"What do you mean?" Jenni propped the basket between herself and the doorjamb.

"The lady is a busybody. She wants to know every detail of your life. That's why I do my laundry at midnight." Myra sat down on the sofa with a cup of tea.

Jenni laughed. "Maybe she's lonely. Be back in an hour or so."

Jenni filled three washers, placed the coins in the slots, and slid them forward. As the washers filled with water, she pulled two chairs together, facing each other. Sitting in one and propping her feet up on the other, she opened her book.

"Well, hello, dear." Jenni peeked over her book to see the petite red-haired woman in a bright yellow short set, her bracelets jingling while she walked.

"Hello, Mrs. Pollard." Jenni kept the book in front of her, hoping her landlady would take the hint.

"I don't think I would put my feet on the chair, dear." Mrs. Pollard was standing beside her.

Jenni smiled and dropped her feet to the floor. Mrs. Pollard sat down in the vacant chair. It looked like she was here to stay, so Jenni put the book in her lap. *Might as well have a little conversation.*

"Did Trey get your ceiling fan fixed, dear?" Mrs. Pollard's heavy makeup and bright red lipstick only accentuated the wrinkles of her leathery, sun-tanned face.

"Yes, ma'am, he did." It had been so long ago, Jenni had almost forgotten.

"Trey is such a good boy, don't you think?"

Jenni chuckled to herself. It was hard to imagine anyone calling Trey a boy with his six-foot-two-inch stature. "I think Trey is very nice. And I'm sure he's a big help to you."

"Oh, yes, dear. During the summers he sometimes helps me with the flowers and does little odd jobs for the tenants. He's very handy, you know." Jenni smiled and nodded her agreement. "Of course, during the regular teaching year he doesn't have so much time. You understand, don't you, dear?"

Jenni nodded again as Mrs. Pollard continued to praise her nephew. "He's such a good person. Oh, and he adores those children that he teaches. Have you met them?" She didn't wait for an answer. "Sometimes the older boy comes with him. Let's see, I think his name is Stephen." Mrs. Pollard continued to talk as Jenni transferred her clothes from washer to dryer. Suddenly a statement caught her attention.

"What did you say?" She quickly sat back down across from Mrs. Pollard.

"About what, dear?"

"About Trey and church?"

"Oh, I said I wish he would get back in church. He used to love church."

Jenni leaned forward. "You mean Trey used to go to church with you?"

"Oh, not with me, dear. He grew up in church. In fact, before the accident, he was studying to become a—"

"Mrs. Pollard, there you are! I've been looking everywhere for you." A young woman holding a baby on one hip and guiding a toddler with her free hand stood in the doorway.

"Well, hello, Lena. Oh, and how are these little dears?" Mrs. Pollard was out of her chair, patting the cheeks of the toddler.

"My kitchen sink is clogged," Lena said. "I called the office but you weren't there."

"Well, let's see, dear." She turned to Jenni. "It was so nice chatting with you, dear." With that comment she was out the door, walking down the veranda with Lena, talking all the while, her bracelets jingling.

Jenni sat alone, trying to digest the information. So Trey used to go to church. She suspected as much. That would explain his knowledge of Scripture. And the accident must have been his sister's car wreck. But what else was Mrs. Pollard going to say when Lena interrupted? And how could she help Trey over his bitterness and bring him back to God? She had to find a way.

❧

After her performance Jenni dressed quickly and went to the

lobby to meet Trey. Tonight he had brought a friend with him, a young man with Down syndrome who helped with the younger children at school. Trey had promised him the night out weeks earlier as a birthday present. Jenni was nervous about meeting him. What if she said the wrong thing? Or worse, what if she reacted the way she had at school? Trying to calm herself, she recalled Trey's saying that Stephen enjoyed listening to classical music. That was encouraging.

She said a silent prayer. *Lord, I'm trying. Please help me tonight.* She found the two of them close to the door, deep in conversation. Stephen was short and stocky, the top of his head barely reaching Trey's shoulder. Trey turned around as she came toward them.

"Jenni, you were great, as usual."

"I think you're prejudiced."

"You're right," he said with a wink. Turning to the young man, he continued. "I want you to meet a good friend of mine, Stephen Barnes. Stephen, this is Jenni Lawson."

Stephen extended his thick hand with a smile. His eyes had an upward slant to them. "Hello, Jenni. I really liked the show."

"Thank you, Stephen. I'm glad you came." She hoped that neither Stephen nor Trey noticed the slight trembling of her own hand as she reached for Stephen's. "So today is your birthday?"

"That's right. I'm twenty-one!"

"Congratulations!"

"I told my mom I was old enough to have my own apartment now," Stephen said as he turned toward Trey.

"I'll bet she didn't like that, did she?" Trey asked.

"No, you know my mom. I was just teasing her, though. I don't really want to move. Not yet anyway," he added with a chuckle.

Stephen's comments surprised Jenni. Not only did he speak, but he carried on a normal conversation. He slurred a few words, but for the most part she had no trouble understanding him.

Trey reached his arm around Jenni's waist. "Why don't you come have pizza with Stephen and me and help us celebrate?"

Jenni felt a little panic rise in her. Trey didn't tell her they would be having dinner together. "Oh, no, I don't want to intrude. You go ahead."

"You wouldn't be intruding, would she, Stephen?"

"No, I'd like for you to come with us. You're a lot prettier than Trey."

Jenni smiled at the comment but still felt uncomfortable. She didn't want to go and was a little angry that Trey was pushing her. Yet she knew he was trying to help her overcome a fear and to understand people with developmental disabilities. She could even sympathize with his efforts, because she also wanted to help Trey get past his anger and bitterness toward God. She also knew she had to make the effort to understand a world that was unfamiliar to her. "Okay. I'd love to go," she said, hoping she sounded more enthusiastic than she felt.

The three of them found a table in the corner of the restaurant and ordered pizza and salad.

"Their salad can't compare to Stephen's." Stephen beamed at Trey's compliment.

"You cook?" Jenni asked with surprise.

"Just a little."

"He makes the best homemade salad dressing you have ever tasted," Trey added.

"I'm impressed. I've never fixed homemade salad dressing in my life."

"My grandmother taught me," Stephen said with pride.

"Trey told me that you help teach the younger children at school," Jenni said, trying to make conversation with Stephen.

Stephen nodded his agreement.

"The kids love Stephen. They fight over who gets to sit beside him," Trey said.

Jenni sipped a soft drink, surprised that she was beginning to relax around Stephen. "What do you teach?" she asked with genuine interest.

"I just help them with their assignments for the day. I like helping them, especially in music class."

Trey got up from the table. "Anyone care to join me at the salad bar for seconds?"

Stephen and Jenni declined and continued their conversation. She actually wanted to know more about him and the children. He was nothing like she had imagined. In fact, she wondered what she really had imagined. Stephen was sociable, polite, and obviously responsible if he helped with the children at school. Why should she be uncomfortable with him?

"Stephen, what is music class like?"

"Oh, we listen to music and the teacher tries to get the kids to sing sometimes, but they always want to dance. It's real funny sometimes."

"I'll bet it is. Do you have music every day?"

"No, I think it's twice a week. I can't remember for sure."

"So the kids would rather dance than sing?" Jenni's interest was piqued slightly.

"Yeah, especially Chrissy."

"What's this about Chrissy?" Trey was back with his plate piled high.

"I told Jenni that Chrissy likes to dance all the time."

"That's right. They all love music, but you can't keep Chrissy still. She seems to be a natural."

"Does she take dance lessons?"

"No, she just has a feel for the music. Even though Chrissy doesn't speak, she expresses herself beautifully with music, doesn't she, Stephen?"

"Yes, and she gets mad if you won't let her dance."

"That's true. She does have that minor behavior problem." Trey smiled. "She would rather dance than work."

"I wish she could see Jenni dance," Stephen said.

"She would like that, except she would want to be up on stage with her."

The pizza came and the conversation changed to things like

everyone's dislike of anchovies and love for onions, and without knowing when it happened, Jenni realized she was completely at ease around Stephen. In fact, she actually enjoyed talking with him and looked forward to meeting him again. She even found herself wondering about Chrissy's love for dancing.

Stephen said good night to Jenni as he got out of the car at his house. Trey walked to the door with him, his arm around his shoulders. It had not been difficult to see how much Stephen admired Trey. It shone from his eyes. And Trey looked on Stephen as a true friend. It was, indeed, a unique relationship, and Jenni respected both young men and their friendship. Again, she had to question her own values. Was she capable of this type of friendship? Could she treat someone with a lower ability with the same respect that Trey showed Stephen?

Trey was back in the car. "Well, what did you think of Stephen?"

"I love your subtle questions."

Trey laughed aloud. "I'm sorry, I was just curious."

"I liked him, I really did. He wasn't at all what I expected."

Trey pulled the car out of the drive and started toward Jenni's apartment. "What did you expect?"

"I don't know. I've been trying to figure that out myself. I guess I didn't expect him to carry on a normal conversation or to find that he had the same interests as other people. He's a remarkable person."

"Perhaps more than you think."

"How's that?"

"Well, Stephen not only helps with the children during the mornings, but he works as a sacker in a grocery store in the afternoons. And he has won his fair share of medals at Special Olympics, even the nationals."

"Do most people with Down syndrome have Stephen's potential?"

"Many do. People with Down syndrome are just like everyone else. They are all unique and have different levels of learning. But with early intervention and better educational programs such as mainstreaming and inclusion, people with disabilities are reaching higher potentials than anyone ever imagined. I'm excited."

"I can tell."

"I'm sorry—"

"No, I was just teasing. What's an early intervention program?"

"Well, studies show that the first three years of a child's life are the most important learning years."

"You mean any child, not just a disabled child?"

"Right, but it's even more important with a child that is developmentally delayed. If we can get these kids into a program soon after birth and just bombard them with stimulation and give them lots of therapy, it makes a big difference. We're actually seeing that difference."

Jenni was silent.

"Hey, I'm boring you. You should never get me started on programs for people with disabilities. I never know when to quit."

"No, it's interesting. Frankly, I'm amazed. I have never heard about programs like that. In fact, I never really thought about it. Does that make me sound uncaring?"

"Of course not. Most people aren't aware of these programs unless they have a family member who is disabled or work with disabled people in some way."

"I think it's wonderful that you and others like you are so dedicated to helping. And Stephen adores you. I can tell."

"Don't put a halo on me, Jenni. We all have something we care deeply about and this happens to be mine."

"Well, I still think you're great."

"Then I'm flattered," he said with a big smile.

They were nearing Jenni's apartment.

"Don't forget we have a date for the beach in the morning," Trey said. "I'll pick you up bright and early."

"How bright and early?"

"Early! I want you to see the sunrise."

"I'd like that. But don't forget I have—"

"A short rehearsal tomorrow afternoon," Trey finished her sentence.

Jenni laughed. "You know my schedule pretty well, don't you?"

"I should. I've been following it for nearly two months."

Trey pulled into the parking lot and walked upstairs with Jenni.

"I guess Myra is still out," Jenni said, stepping into the dimly lit apartment.

Trey pulled her into his arms and kissed her lips softly at first, then harder. He held her so close she could feel his heart beating against her. He kissed her face, neck, then his lips found hers again and Jenni responded with a passion she had never felt before. Suddenly she pulled away from him and Trey tilted his head back and took a deep, uneven breath.

"You'd better go," she said, her voice a little shaky.

Trey took Jenni's hands in his and brushed his lips over her forehead and hair. She closed her eyes and leaned against his chest, feeling the warmth of his body through his shirt. He took hold of her shoulders and held her slightly away from him. The outside light filtered through the window. Jenni looked searchingly into his eyes. She was certain he loved her as much as she loved him, but he only said good night and walked away.

Jenni leaned her back against the closed door and gave a long sigh. Then she walked over to the window without turning on the light and watched Trey's car leave the parking lot. Suddenly she felt very tired and knew it had little to do with her dancing. She showered and crawled into bed, trying to sort out all the feelings inside of her.

fifteen

The colors on the horizon changed from shades of purple to orange to yellow as the sun appeared to rise out of the Atlantic Ocean. The cool damp sand squished under Jenni's bare feet as she and Trey walked along the beach. Jenni felt like she was in paradise—beautiful sunrises, gentle waves splashing upon the sand, and sea oats blowing in the breeze. But most of all, the tall blond man at her side.

"Why so quiet?" Trey asked.

"Just enjoying all of this." She threw her hands up in a motion to encompass the world around her. "Isn't it beautiful? I love Florida. I wish I never had to leave."

"You don't have to."

Trey took the beach towel from off his shoulder and spread it on the sand. They sat watching the ocean, now glistening under the bright sun. Jenni knew the question Trey was thinking before he finally asked.

"Did you check on that ballet company in Orlando?"

"No." Jenni stared out over the wide expanse of water.

"Why not?"

"Because it's not what I want." She turned to face him.

"You just said that you wished you never had to leave Florida. So why won't you check into Ballet Shekinah?"

"Trey, you just wouldn't understand." Jenni pulled her knees up under her chin and wrapped her arms around her legs. She looked back out over the water, squinting from the bright sunlight.

"Try me." Agitated, Trey stood up and paced a couple of steps away, then back. "It's a Christian ballet company. I thought that would please you, yet you won't even go talk with them."

"Would it make you feel better if I called them?" Jenni was irritated that Trey was trying to interfere in her professional career.

"If you're not interested, no."

"Good. I'm not interested. Satisfied?" She looked up at him.

Trey sat down beside her. "But why? I mean, you want me to go to church, so why don't you want to work for a Christian company?"

Jenni took a long breath and let out a sigh. "I have worked all my life on ballet. I have. . .goals and dreams."

"Like what?"

"Every ballerina dreams of being with a metropolitan company like the New York City Ballet. It's what we work toward."

"How does Ballet Shekinah fit into this?"

"It doesn't. That's the point. Do you want me to give up my dreams?" She looked at him questioningly.

Trey thought awhile. "No, I don't think so." He ran his fingers through his hair and turned toward her. "Well, maybe I do if it means your being in New York instead of Florida." Jenni stared at him in dismay. "Hear me out. Maybe I just don't understand ballet, but if it's the dance you love so much and you want to honor God, as you've said, then wouldn't the Christian company do that better than the metropolitan?"

"You're right about one thing. You don't understand," Jenni said with frustration. She lay back on the towel and turned over on her stomach, letting the sun warm her back.

"Okay. Obviously, I don't understand. But the best I can tell, Oklahoma City isn't any closer to New York City than Orlando."

"But it's a metropolitan ballet."

"Why are you really going back to Oklahoma?"

"I just told you. My job."

"And what else besides the job?"

Jenni jerked herself up to a sitting position. "What do you mean?"

"I guess I'm asking if there is someone in Oklahoma waiting

for you." Trey was very solemn.

Jenni thought about Doug and the letters he had been writing, asking her to come home. "Not. . .now. No, I'm not going back to anyone."

"What do you mean, 'not now'?"

She looked over at Trey, who hadn't taken his eyes off her face since he asked the question. "Why are you asking me this?"

"Because I want to know." There was no smile on his face, and she knew she might as well tell him about Doug.

"Okay. I was involved with someone before I left, but that relationship is over."

"Why do you say that?"

Because I'm in love with you, she wanted to shout, but instead answered, "I'm not in love with him."

"Were you before you left?" Trey sat cross-legged, arms propped up, his chin resting on his fists in front of him.

"I didn't know. I guess that was one of the reasons I was anxious to get a job so far away. I knew the separation would tell me what I needed to know." She brushed sand from her legs.

"And?"

"And. . .I found out." She looked over at Trey.

"But it might be different when you go back. Will he still be there?"

"I suppose so. But it won't make any difference."

Trey stretched out on his side, propping himself up on one elbow. "How can you be sure of that?"

She hesitated, not knowing whether to tell him of her feelings about finding the right person to marry. Still, she wanted him to understand that she was not going back to Doug.

"I don't know if you will understand this, but I know I won't go back to Doug because he isn't God's choice for me. You see, I never really thought I was in love with him, but I wasn't sure. He's a good person and a fine Christian man. And he thought I would. . ."

"Would what?"

Jenni sighed. "He thought I would marry him one day. But now I know that I'm not in love with him, in fact never was, and that he isn't God's choice for me."

"You really believe God has a special person for you?"

"Yes, I do." She thought about Trey's angry outburst during their discussion at the beach and hoped that didn't happen now.

"And do you know who that person is?" He seemed more curious than irritated.

Jenni turned her head away from Trey as she watched the few white wisps of clouds float through the blue sky. Seagulls flew over the water, squawking and swooping down occasionally.

"No," she finally answered softly. "But God knows, and He will show me."

Trey didn't respond. She wished his mind weren't so closed to a discussion about God. He lay on the sand, eyes closed. Jenni decided he was asleep and leaned over close to him. Suddenly he grabbed her and pulled her over to him in a wrestling, teasing manner. They were laughing again and the serious conversation was left behind.

Finally Jenni scrambled to her feet. "I have an idea. Let's—"

"No, Jenni, no! I'm not going to look for shells again. I have scavenged this beach from one end to the other with you all summer and I absolutely refuse to look for another shell."

"I wasn't even going to suggest that." She laughed at his shocked expression. "Let's go to the souvenir shop at the pier."

Trey groaned. "I'm supposed to be excited about looking at T-shirts and coffee mugs with Florida scrawled all over them?"

"But it's fun!"

"No, it's not. Besides, I have a better idea. Why don't I haul out that picnic food from the car?"

"Don't men ever think of anything besides food?"

"Well, at the moment I can think of one other thing. And

that's a particular dark-haired, brown-eyed beauty." He was on his feet, arms circled around her.

"Never mind," Jenni said, feeling a warm blush, even in the hot sun. "I've suddenly developed a tremendous appetite, too. But I still plan to go to the pier when we finish eating."

❧

Jenni walked down aisles filled with souvenir trinkets. Corded net and starfish were draped on walls, and T-shirts with every message imaginable hung on walls and racks all around the shop. She examined personalized coffee cups.

"Now I might be able to handle this one," Trey said, holding up a mug with "Boss" written on it.

Jenni waved him away.

"Aw, come on, Jenni." He picked up a T-shirt covered with a tropical scene that had "Cocoa Beach" stamped on the bottom of it. "This is tourist stuff."

They walked to the back of the store, where shelves were lined with shells. "Okay, that's it. I'm not looking at shells." Trey caught Jenni's arm and started to pull her away.

"Wait, Trey." She picked up a basket filled with assorted shells and starfish. "I think my mother would like this."

"Fine. Get it and let's go."

"Oh, look!" Trey rolled his eyes upward and turned to walk away. "Trey!" She pulled him over to a basket of sand dollars. "I've always wanted to find a sand dollar on the beach. Oh, look! Aren't those painted ones pretty?"

"I have to admit I like those. Sometimes I keep a box of small sand dollars at the school. The kids love them because they're so hard to find on the beach and when you do find one, it's usually broken. So when they work real hard, I give them one."

"Are they painted?"

"I'm a speech pathologist, not an artist."

"I used to paint a little. In fact, Myra paints, too, when she has time."

"Good. Let's go."

"Maybe I could paint some for your kids. I'm sure Myra wouldn't mind if I used some of her acrylics." Jenni found some medium-sized sand dollars. "How many? Still eight?"

"Counting Ryan, who's home with a broken leg, yes."

She counted out a full dozen. "Just in case I break some," she smiled. "Help me carry them."

Trey grabbed a basket from the end of the aisle. "You're serious?"

"Do you think they would like them?"

"Sure, but it seems like a lot of work."

"I'll let you know when I've finished them and you can pick them up."

"Or you could bring them."

Jenni turned to face him. Strange how her feelings could change so quickly. Painting for the children seemed fun, but seeing them. . . "No. I can't do that."

"Jenni, you've got to try. You did fine with Stephen."

But Stephen didn't grab me or scream, she thought to herself.

"Never mind. I'll pick them up," he said.

"I'm sorry. I just don't think I can handle it."

"How are you going to know if you don't try?"

"Would you be with me?"

"I'll always be with you," Trey said softly.

Taken off guard, Jenni caught her breath on the word "always" and stuttered, "Uh, when do. . .when should. . . okay, I'll try."

"Good. Let's get out of here."

❧

The kitchen table was covered with painted sand dollars. Each one had a scene of the ocean and beach. She had meticulously added sea oats, palm trees, or seagulls. Jenni hoped the children would enjoy the vividly colored scenes. She had painted one for Trey with the sun rising over the ocean, knowing how much he liked to watch the first rays of orange and yellow rise above and stretch across the blue water of the Atlantic.

She heard footsteps on the stairs outside and ran back to the bedroom to put away Trey's sand dollar. She would give it to him at the end of the summer. She opened the door and led Trey into the kitchen.

"What do you think?"

"They're great! I never dreamed you were going to go into such detail." He picked up one and examined it. "You even have little shells on the beach. And the colors. . .I don't know what to say. I thought you were just going to do a little beach scene—you know, ocean and sand. They're great. I don't know what else to say." Trey put his arms around Jenni and hugged her close.

"You think the kids will be pleased?"

"They'll love them. Now do you still want to come to the school?"

"I don't know," she said, turning back to look at the sand dollars on the table.

Trey looked at her with soft blue eyes.

"Okay, I'll try. When?"

"How about tomorrow? They have music and it's always a fun time for them. You could watch them dance."

"I'll drop by a little before nine."

"I'll watch for you and meet you at the front entrance."

"Okay."

Trey took Jenni's hands and pulled her to him and looked directly into her brown eyes. "I know the kids will love you and I think you'll feel the same about them once you get to know them. But I don't want you upset, so don't do this just for me. Do it for you."

Jenni nodded her agreement. "I admit I'm still scared."

"Don't forget, I'll be right beside you."

He pulled her into his arms, and Jenni laid her head against his chest. *Dear God,* she prayed silently, *if Trey isn't Your choice for my life, then take away these feelings that make me long to be with him and thrill to his touch. Take away the desire to spend the rest of my life with him.*

sixteen

Jenni's apprehension began to mount as she drove into the parking lot at the school. Trey came out the door and jogged up the sidewalk to meet her.

"You nervous?"

Jenni nodded.

"Bet you'll surprise yourself. You'll probably enjoy the kids, then wonder what had you scared."

"I hope so."

"Here's something for good luck." He kissed her quickly while she held the car door open for him to pick up the box of sand dollars.

"Trey!"

"Don't worry. No one is watching."

They walked into the building and down the hall to the music class. Jenni thought about her encounter with Russell and Tanya and felt her pulse quicken. What if she acted the same way in music class? She could hear the noise from outside the door.

"What are they doing?"

"Right now *they* are playing the music. They think they're great," Trey said with a smile. "In a little while Karen will put on a tape and let them dance. That's the part you'll like."

All Jenni could do was nod in agreement, take a deep breath, and say a silent prayer as they entered the room.

The music room had two bright yellow walls with windows on one end and mirrors along one wall. A piano dominated one corner. She was surprised to see how much it resembled the rooms where she had taken so many dance lessons.

The children were marching around the room playing simple musical instruments, such as tambourines and horns.

Some of them gave a quick wave or special smile as they saw Trey.

"Where are Tanya and Russell?" she asked after they were seated in folding chairs near the door.

"Oh, I should have told you. Russell goes to another program two days a week for older children, so he misses music. And Tanya gets too upset with the noise. Then Ryan is homebound right now, so all we have are the five little ones for music. I'm sure it's easier for Karen because Stephen can help a lot with the younger kids."

At the teacher's request the children put their horns, tambourines, and bells into a box and ran back to the center of the room clapping and giggling. She turned on the tape player and began some simple rhythm movements. Jenni watched as each little person imitated the movement. She saw Stephen bring back a little boy who strayed away from the group. Soon they had their arms out, turning in circles and wiggling their bodies to the rhythm of the music. Though they were awkward, Jenni was surprised by their movements.

"Well, what do you think?" Trey took one of her cold hands and clasped it between his own.

"They're really dancing," she said, trying to smile.

The music ended and she and Trey clapped for the performance. The children turned and bowed after some prodding from Karen.

"I'm surprised," she said.

Suddenly the children all clamored around Trey. "Hey, you guys are getting good." He wrestled playfully with them.

They all smiled their appreciation. One child crawled into his lap, and others were hanging onto his arms and around his neck. *Oh, please don't let them hug me,* Jenni pleaded silently.

Chrissy came and stood directly in front of Jenni, looking rather intent.

"Chrissy, you are a lovely dancer," Jenni said as she put her hand out to her, not knowing what else to do. Chrissy ignored the hand and threw her arms around Jenni's neck. Startled, she immediately wanted to pull away but fought the impulse and tried to concentrate on Chrissy's openness and innocent love.

Chrissy released her hold as quickly as she had grabbed her, then a little boy dressed in red jogging shorts and white T-shirt walked over to Jenni.

"You smell good."

"Well, thank you."

Another pointed to the box and asked, "What's that?"

Trey got their attention. "Be real quiet and I'll tell you what's in the box. This is my friend Jenni and she made something special for you." A few turned their eyes toward Jenni, but the others watched the box. "Be sure to say thank you when Jenni gives you the surprise, and be very careful. They can break."

Jenni passed out the painted sand dollars and watched the children's faces light up as they saw the pictures. One little girl lingered near her, chattering away, though Jenni couldn't understand what she said.

"Pretty," commented another child as she hugged Jenni's waist. It wasn't clear whether she meant the sand dollar or Jenni. She stiffened a little at the child's embrace.

Trey's voice boomed over the children. "Where are my hugs? I carried the box." All the children ran to Trey and he smiled and winked in Jenni's direction, obviously pleased. Jenni was relieved that the children's attention was on Trey. Stephen walked over to her.

"They all like Trey," he said.

"I can tell. It's good to see you again, Stephen."

"Did you paint those?"

"Yes, I did." She reached into the box and took out one with a sailboat, blue water, and a sandy beach with seagulls. She handed it to Stephen.

Stephen's eyes lit up. "Jenni, are you sure you want me to have this? It's so pretty. Don't you want to keep it?"

"I have others. Besides, I painted that one especially for you."

"Thank you." Stephen surprised Jenni with a hug, then made his way over to Trey to show him the painted sand dollar. She could see the little boy pride and love that had never left Stephen and realized that it was not at all unattractive. In fact, it was the opposite, yet she still was uncomfortable.

Chrissy again stood in front of Jenni, looking up into her face.

"Do you like it?" Jenni pointed to the sand dollar.

Chrissy nodded.

"Do you like to dance?" Jenni tried to do movements to mimic dancing.

Again Chrissy nodded, then walked back to the other children. Jenni was thinking about Chrissy's lack of speech when Trey brought the music teacher over to meet her.

"Jenni, this is Karen Thompson. Karen, Jenni Lawson. She dances at the Civic Theater."

"I know, I've seen you perform," Karen said to Jenni. "You're very talented."

"Thank you. I'm impressed with your teaching. The children do very well."

"Thanks. I think they're great. They tend to have a natural rhythm about them and they absolutely love music and dancing. I just wish I could spend more time with them."

"Karen does this during her free time," Trey added to the conversation.

"It's no sacrifice," Karen quickly added. "I love working with them, although it's getting a little awkward for the two of us." She laughed, patting her pregnant stomach. "But I can work a little longer. We'll just have more song than dance. I'd better get back to the kids. Nice talking with you, Jenni."

"Thank you for letting me visit."

"Anytime. You're always welcome." Karen walked away, calling the children to a circle in the center of the room, then put on another tape.

As Trey and Jenni turned to go, Jenni ran head-on into a little boy, knocking him to the floor. Trey picked him up immediately. "Patrick, you okay? You'd better go over there with the other kids and Mrs. Thompson."

Patrick's large brown eyes were magnified through thick glasses. He stared at Jenni, then hugged her tightly. She stood absolutely still, then tried to pry the child away, but he squeezed her tighter.

"Excuse me," she said, pulling the boy away from her. Trey took Patrick to the center of the room as Jenni quickly slipped out the door. She was trembling when Trey joined her in the hall.

"Come on." He led her through PT to the small room where he had speech therapy. There was a table and two chairs, Trey's desk, and shelves lined with miniature objects and trays of cards.

"What happened to you?" He took her shaking hands in his.

"He wouldn't let go of me."

"Sweetheart, don't you think you're overreacting?"

"Of course I'm overreacting. Do you think this is intentional?" She pulled her shaking hands away and turned toward the window.

"They're just kids, Jenni."

"I know that!" She turned and faced him, almost in tears.

Trey paced the small room and ran his fingers through his hair. "Well, can't you do something?"

"What would you suggest?"

"I don't know!"

Jenni's fear was now turning to anger. "You were the one who asked me to come. You said you would support me."

"And I am supporting you. At least, I'm trying. It's just that your fears seem so. . .illogical."

"Illogical! Thanks for all your understanding!" Jenni turned to go.

Trey took her arm. "Wait. I didn't mean it like that."

"Then what did you mean? I find it strange that you can have your own prejudices and irrational ideas, but it's not *logical* for me."

"What ideas are you talking about?"

"Your ideas about God. I personally find them illogical, to use your term."

"Don't start, Jenni."

"I didn't start anything."

"I'm not going to argue."

"Argue! You think an argument is what I want? Understanding is what I want. It's what you promised me when you asked me to come." She jerked the door open and walked out.

"Jenni!" Trey followed her to the PT room, where the therapist looked up in surprise.

"Don't bother. I can find my own way out." Jenni made her way out to the hall and ran out of the building.

❧

Jenni and Myra were finishing the dishes when they heard a knock at the door.

"I'll get it." Jenni grabbed a towel, drying her hands as she crossed the room and opened the door. Trey stood in the doorway. Jenni crossed her arms over her chest in front of her. "What do you want?"

"May I come in?" he said, walking past her.

"Why ask? You're already inside." She glared at him from across the room.

"Well, I could leave if I make you that uncomfortable."

"No one's stopping you." Jenni held the door open.

Myra came out of the kitchen. "Time out, you two. Jenni, I'm going to the grocery store. Trey, I would suggest a little more diplomacy on your part." She grabbed her purse and went out the door, closing it behind her.

Trey placed a small wrapped package on the coffee table. "I guess she's right."

Jenni didn't speak or move.

"Look, I'm sorry about this morning." He walked over and

put his arms around her. "I let you down. You were right to walk out."

Jenni pulled herself out of his embrace. "You don't have any idea how hard that trip was for me."

"No, I don't. But I know I should have been more understanding." He put his arms around her again and hugged her to him. "Sweetheart, I wish I could make all your fears disappear."

Jenni laced her arms around his waist. "I told you I couldn't handle it."

Trey held her at arm's length from himself and looked directly into her eyes. "That's not true. You *did* handle it. Yes, you got a little upset once, but you still did it. You're trying."

Jenni started to walk away but he pulled her back. "I don't know, Trey. Maybe I'm like my mother. Maybe I won't ever get over this."

"Nonsense. You made a great start today."

"That's not what you said at school." She looked up at him.

"I know. And I think I apologized for that." Trey picked up the package from the coffee table and handed it to her. "I bought something for you."

Jenni held the package for a while, staring at the white paper and red ribbon.

"Well, open it!"

"You shouldn't be giving me gifts. What's the occasion?"

"Would you just open it and stop worrying about an occasion?"

She tore at the paper and opened the box. "Oh, Trey, it's beautiful!" She lifted out a hand-carved wooden music box. The top had costumed children that danced and twirled to the tune of "It's a Small World." "I've never seen anything like it and I love music boxes. You shouldn't have, but I'm so glad you did. I love it!"

"Well, I knew you liked that tourist stuff." Trey smiled.

She stood on her toes and gave him a quick kiss. "Thank you. Now, wait right here."

"Where are you going?"

"Just a minute," she called back from the bedroom, then walked into the living room, hands behind her back. "I have something for you."

"What?"

"I was going to give this to you right before I left for Oklahoma, but I think I'd rather do it now." She handed him a glass case containing the sand dollar she had painted with the brilliant sunrise reflecting its colors across the ocean.

Trey stared at the gift for a long while, saying nothing.

"I knew how much you loved the ocean at sunrise," Jenni said, not sure what to think of his silence.

Trey hugged her so hard she could hardly breathe. "Oh, Jenni, you can't go back to Oklahoma. I wouldn't know what to do without you."

seventeen

Sounds of Christian praise choruses drifted down the corridor as Jenni made her way toward the dance studio of Ballet Shekinah. Without Trey's knowledge, she had watched a performance the week before and called the director for an interview. Realizing she was almost half an hour early, she slipped into the studio to watch rehearsal, hoping she didn't disturb anyone or draw attention to herself. She quietly sat down on the floor, cross-legged, and watched as the dancers worked on a dance variation to a song that praised the names of God.

A petite woman with dark auburn hair twisted into a bun counted time and worked on choreography. "Okay, let's put it all together now. Start at the top, go straight through, then we'll take a break."

Jenni watched the fluid movements, again surprised—as she had been the week before—at the professionalism before her. She had to admit that these people were excellent dancers. *I wonder why they aren't in a metropolitan ballet company,* she thought to herself.

"Okay, great. Do some stretches, then take a break." The auburn-haired woman walked toward her. Jenni got to her feet immediately. "Jenni Lawson?" She was patting her face with a towel.

Jenni extended her hand. "Yes, and you must be Marilyn Myers."

"Just Lyn. That's what everyone calls me," she said, shaking Jenni's hand. "Let's go to my office where we can hear a little better." She glanced over her shoulder at the dancers stretching, talking, and laughing. "We're kind of informal around here. Professional, but informal."

Jenni followed Lyn into a small room with a desk, file

cabinet, blackboard, a few straight-back chairs near the window, and a small refrigerator. She took two boxes of orange juice from the refrigerator and offered one to Jenni. "It's not the height of luxury, but it's quiet."

"Oh, it's fine." Jenni took the juice and sat down. "I hope you don't mind my observing. I was a little early and couldn't resist. That dance variation was great, and I love the music. It must be nice to dance to Christian music."

"It is. That's one of the pluses in our company. Also, since we're a small company and have the same beliefs, we are more like a family than a company. You could probably tell that." Jenni nodded in agreement. "Have you seen a performance?" Lyn came right to the point.

"Yes, last week."

"What did you think?"

"I liked it. I don't think I've ever seen anything like it. The Christian music, I mean, and the testimonies of faith."

"How do you feel about that, Jenni?"

"I. . .I don't know," Jenni said, taken off guard by the question.

"What is your interest in Ballet Shekinah?"

"Well, as I said on the phone, I'm dancing at the Civic Theater in Cocoa Beach for the summer. I plan to return to Oklahoma when the summer ends, but my friend told me about your company, so I thought I'd check into it."

"Are you a Christian?"

"Yes." Jenni found Lyn's open manner somewhat intimidating. She almost felt like she had to defend herself, yet she didn't know why.

"I realize I'm being pretty blunt, Jenni, but we have lots of people interested in our company. We have to make sure a person wants to join us for the right reason."

"What is the right reason?"

Lyn finished her juice and leaned back in her chair. "Before I tell you that, why don't you tell me about yourself. When did you start dancing? Where? What are your ambitions?

Why do you dance? That sort of thing."

Jenni looked at her in surprise. Lyn laughed. "Relax, Jenni. I don't mean to interrogate you, really. Just tell me why you like to dance."

Jenni held the half-empty box of juice in her hands. Her gaze drifted to the palm-shaded window showing a cloudless blue sky. How could she answer such a complicated question? Finally, she turned to Lyn. "I don't really know why I love to dance. I just know something inside me would die without it." She put the box on the desk beside her, using her hands to help express what she felt. She crossed her hands over her heart. "It's like God put something deep in my soul that can only be expressed when I dance. When I'm lonely, I dance. When I'm happy, I dance. I don't know how else to answer."

Lyn rested her chin on her hand, propping her elbow on the desk, a smile on her face. "That's beautifully said."

Jenni smiled. "I've never had an interview like this one."

"That's because we're not like most companies. Our main purpose and desire at Ballet Shekinah is to honor and glorify God. I believe dancing is a gift from God. I want to use that gift to praise and glorify Him. Everyone in our company feels the same. Do you feel that way, Jenni?"

"I never thought about it quite that way, but yes, that's exactly what I want to do with my dance."

"I thought so." Lyn walked across the small room and pulled a second juice from the refrigerator, offering Jenni another.

"No, thanks."

"So what do we need to talk about?" Lyn asked. "Are you interested in joining our company? Do you want to know more about us? What actually brings you here?"

"Good question," Jenni answered. "I'll be honest with you. I don't know that I would want to join your company, but I'd like to know more about it."

Lyn got up. "Come with me." She led Jenni to a room equipped with a TV, VCR, and other video equipment. She popped a tape into the recorder. A couple danced across the screen. "This is Helena and Bryan. They're married and came from the Chicago Ballet." Jenni's mouth dropped open in surprise. Lyn fast-forwarded the tape. "Sasha comes from Yugoslavia." She continued through the tape. Everyone came from a professional ballet company.

Lyn turned to Jenni. "Surprised?"

"Well. . .yes. Why did they quit?"

"They didn't quit. They just changed companies."

"But. . ."

"You're still early in your career, Jenni. Your greatest desire is probably to be in the New York City Ballet. Am I right?"

Jenni flushed a little. "I suppose."

"I understand. That was my desire, too. In fact, I made it."

Jenni looked at her in amazement.

"And you can, too, if you want it badly enough. You're good enough." She smiled at Jenni's puzzled expression. "I've seen you perform."

"Oh, great. Now you tell me."

Lyn laughed. "Don't worry. You were very good. In fact, I think you know how good you are, don't you? You have a dream, right?"

"You understand that?"

Lyn nodded in agreement.

"Is there anything wrong with that?"

"Of course not."

"Then why did you quit, or change, as you call it? How could you give up what you worked for all your life?"

"Because I wasn't fulfilled doing what I was doing. I couldn't share my faith with my audience the way I wanted to do." Jenni was silent. "It's hard to give up a dream, isn't it?" Lyn asked. Jenni nodded silently. "You don't have to give it up, Jenni."

"What do you mean?"

"Maybe Ballet Shekinah isn't for you. Maybe you really are meant for New York or Chicago. Being a Christian doesn't mean you have to change your goals, as long as those goals are in line with God's will."

"I'm afraid I would always wonder if I could have made it."

"Then maybe you should go for it."

Jenni glanced at her watch. "Oh, look how long I've kept you. I never intended to stay so long." She turned to leave.

Lyn walked out into the hall with her. "Pray about it, Jenni. You have to go where God leads you. You would be very unhappy with us if this isn't where you want to be."

"Thanks. I appreciate that. But it does seem like a great company."

"It is. And if you do feel God's leading you to us, let me know. I really think we could use you."

"Are you serious?"

"Absolutely. One of our lead dancers is about to take maternity leave, so we're looking for someone. But we want them to be looking for us also." She smiled. "Let's keep in touch."

"I'll do that." Jenni left the building and nearly ran to her car, both from exhilaration and necessity. She barely had time to get to Cocoa Beach for rehearsal. In the car she thought back over the interview. It was a compliment to know that Lyn thought her professional enough to join their company. *Funny,* she thought. *On the way over I thought I was the professional and this was just a little local ballet.* She chuckled to herself. "Wouldn't Trey love to know this?" she said aloud. But she decided not to tell him about the interview. After all, her dream had not changed. She still longed for the metropolitan ballet, but it was an honor to know that Ballet Shekinah might ask her to join them. And that would be hard to keep to herself tonight.

❧

"I'm starved," Trey said as they stopped at an intersection for a red light.

"Me, too. And I love Mexican food, so be prepared."

"Does that mean you're not going to eat that healthy stuff like sprouts and yogurt?"

"Right. Tonight I'm living on the edge."

"How's that?" The light changed and Trey moved forward with the traffic.

"Eating your kind of food." Jenni laughed.

"Hey, that's a cheap shot." Trey glanced at Jenni, who was looking out the side window over her shoulder. "What are you looking at?"

"Oh, I missed where that verse was found." She turned back to face the front.

"What verse? What are you talking about?"

"There was a Bible verse, one of my favorites, on the marquee in front of that church we just passed, and I was trying to see where it was found."

"If it's your favorite, I would think you would know where it's found."

"You would think. But I have a hard time remembering Scripture references. Let's see, 'Delight yourself in the LORD and he will give you the desires of your heart.' Psalm. . . mmm, 34:4, I think."

"Psalm 37:4," Trey said.

"Oh, did you see it?"

"No."

Jenni turned to look at Trey. "If you didn't see it, then how do you know? I think it's Psalm 34:4."

"Right verse, wrong chapter. Psalm 34:4 says, 'I sought the LORD and he heard me, and delivered me from all my fears.' "

Jenni looked surprised. "That's right. I remember now. But how did you know?" She looked at Trey with a puzzled expression.

"Went to Sunday school when I was a kid."

"And did they teach you where to find the book of Habakkuk in Sunday school?" she asked, referring to the church service.

"Of course." Trey turned and gave a quick smile. "You know that little song everybody memorizes about the books of the Bible."

"And you remembered it all these years?"

"Guess so." Trey pulled into the parking lot of the restaurant. "There's John's car. Guess they beat us."

"Trey, how do you know so much about the Bible?"

"I don't."

"Yes, you do. I noticed it at church."

"Jenni, I am not going to discuss theology in front of a restaurant, especially when I'm hungry." Trey had his hand on the door handle.

"Will you discuss it later?"

"Maybe."

John and Cindy were waiting for them inside the foyer. "Hope we haven't kept you waiting," Trey said.

"Just arrived." John shook hands with Trey.

The waiter escorted them to the garden room, which resembled a Mexican courtyard. Trailing bougainvillea crept down full glass windows, and colorful serapes decorated whitewashed walls. They sampled enchiladas, quesadillas, chiles rellenos, and took sopapillas home in a doggie bag.

❧

"I don't think I'll ever be able to eat again." Jenni flipped on the light as they walked into the apartment, then automatically slipped off her shoes.

"Where's Myra?"

"Probably out with Nicholas. They've been seeing a lot of each other lately."

"Are they serious?" Trey sat down on the sofa.

"I don't know. Why?" Jenni sat down beside him, tucking her feet up beside her.

"Just curious. That's a big cultural difference. Didn't you say he was from Russia?"

Jenni nodded. "They get along great. But speaking of differences, what about us?" She had been hoping for an opportunity to resume their previous conversation.

"Neither of us is from Russia, so guess we're okay." Trey turned and smiled at her.

She hit his arm playfully. "You know what I mean. Seriously,

Trey, you tell me you don't believe in God, yet you can quote Bible verses and look up unfamiliar Scripture passages. That doesn't make sense." She didn't want to tell him about her conversation with Mrs. Pollard. She was certain he would not approve of his aunt's discussing his private life.

"Jenni, I don't want to discuss religion."

"But it's important to me."

"Well, I'm sorry, but it's not to me."

"Then I don't see how we can continue our relationship."

Trey stood up and walked to the window and stared out into the night. Jenni watched in silence. He turned back to face her. "Why are you doing this?"

"You said you would discuss it."

"I said 'maybe.' " He ran a hand through his hair, the way he always did when he was angry or irritated.

"Trey, I have to know. The Bible makes it clear that a Christian is not—"

"To marry a non-Christian. 'Be not unequally yoked.' "

"See. There you go again, quoting the Bible. I don't understand."

"Look, Jenni, at one time I believed everything you believe, but not anymore. I used to quote all those verses to people. 'Cast all your care upon Him; for He careth for you.' 1 Peter 5:7. 'I can do all things through Christ who strengthens me.' Philippians 4:13. 'The prayer of faith shall save the sick.' James 5:15. Well, it doesn't work. Nothing saves the sick. Not doctors, not prayers, not even God!" Trey was almost shouting.

"Surely you can't believe that. You're taking things out of context. The Bible says—"

"I *know* what the Bible says." He held his hands up defensively.

Jenni sat quietly, trying to make sense of everything. Trey paced the room a couple of times, then sat down beside her. He put one arm around her and turned her face toward him with the other hand. "Sweetheart, I know you don't understand, but

I just can't explain things to you right now."

"Is it because of what happened to your sister?"

Trey dropped his arms from around her in a hopeless gesture.

"Don't you think I know a little about grief, too? I grew up without a father. He was killed in a plane crash when I was four."

"Now I know why you had never flown before."

"You're changing the subject."

"I'm trying!"

"Trey, you can't keep that bitterness locked inside you. It will destroy you."

"Let me worry about that."

"But—"

Trey put his hand to her lips. "No more. I should never have told you any of this."

She pulled his hand away. "You're wrong. You should have told me a long time ago. And you still need to tell me the rest."

"There is no more. Case closed." He stood up to leave.

"Is that how you handle your problems? Just walk out?"

"You got part of it right. It's *my* problem, not yours."

"But when you—" She caught herself before she said *love*. "When you care about someone, you want to help. Can't I help?"

"Yes. You can quit asking questions and accept me as I am. Is that too hard for you?"

Jenni was on her feet. "I think that's a cruel and sarcastic remark!"

Trey wrapped his arms around her and let out a long sigh. "Yes, it was. I'm sorry. But we can't argue like this, Jenni." He took hold of her chin and tilted her head up, then placed his lips on hers.

Jenni circled her arms around his neck and stood on her toes. Trey pulled his head back and looked at her with troubled blue eyes. "Give me time, Jenni. Give *us* some time." He kissed her again, then said good night and left.

eighteen

Wanting to be sure things were okay with Trey, Jenni decided to stop by the school and say hello before going to her class. She walked into the physical therapy room. "Anne?"

"Yes."

"I'm Jenni Lawson. Is Trey with a student?"

"Oh, I'm afraid you just missed him. He started working with a homebound student today. Would you like me to give him a message?"

"No, thanks. I can talk with him later."

Leaving the room, she heard the sounds of horns and tambourines and voices singing out of tune. She walked down the hall, stepped into the music room, and sat down quietly, hoping not to disturb the class. They were marching around in a circle singing the alphabet song. Karen said something to Stephen and walked over to Jenni.

"Hi. Glad you decided to visit again."

"I hope I'm not interrupting."

"Goodness, no," Karen said, sitting down beside Jenni. "I welcome the break. Stephen can handle them for a few minutes. Did you need anything in particular?"

"No. Actually, I dropped by to see Trey, but he's gone."

"Where is he?"

"Anne said he was with a homebound student."

"Oh, that would be Ryan."

"I think I remember Trey's mentioning him." Jenni looked back at the children. "Chrissy has potential, doesn't she?" Her eyes followed the little girl.

"Jenni," Karen said, then paused. "Why don't you help me with the kids?"

Jenni felt a flush as her heart beat a little harder. "Oh,

Karen, no, I don't think so."

"I think you would enjoy it, and I could certainly use the help. I'm getting so large I feel a little awkward with the dancing. The rest is no problem."

"I don't know anything about teaching."

"You don't have to know much about teaching for this. You dance, they follow. It's that simple. At least they try."

Jenni sat silently.

"Jenni? It was only a suggestion. I probably shouldn't have asked. I know you're very busy. But feel free to come watch anytime." Karen started to get up.

"It's not that." Jenni felt she should explain. "I mean, yes, I'm busy. But I'm sure you are, too, yet you volunteer your time. I just don't know how to work with children."

"Do you want to try?"

Jenni took a deep breath. "I don't know. I have, uh, difficulty being around. . .uh. . ."

"People with disabilities?"

"I know it makes no sense but I have this. . .fear or something. And I can't seem to get over it."

"Let me give you some advice, Jenni. First of all, stop thinking of them as different. Sure, one of them may drool on you, and some can't talk very well or maybe not talk at all. But you'll be accepted and loved even if you don't return it. That's what is so unique about them."

"Karen, I really wish I could do that. It makes me angry at myself that I can't. I've even prayed about it."

"I'm so glad you said that. I'm a Christian, too, so could I be honest with you? I mean really blunt?"

"Sure."

"You need to realize that each one of these children is just as important in this society as you are. Recognize their worth, Jenni. Jesus accepted you with all your flaws and imperfections. Now, maybe to the public you don't seem so imperfect as a disabled person. But to Jesus you're equal. And you have to accept the kids the same way. They're equal to you. They don't need your sympathy or pity, but they need and deserve your love and acceptance."

"You certainly know how to put me in my place."

"I don't mean to offend you, Jenni. But there is a wealth of love waiting for you through these children and others with disabilities. God has given you an exceptional talent. Now He is giving you the opportunity to share it."

"You really think I can do it?"

"I have no doubt. You wouldn't be here if you didn't have a desire hidden deep in your heart. Just think about it." Karen smiled at Jenni and patted her hand.

"Okay. I'll think about it. But right now I've got to get to class." Jenni got up to leave.

"Bet I see you next week," Karen called to Jenni as she walked to the door.

Jenni smiled and waved.

❧

After class and rehearsal Jenni ran by the supermarket and picked up the few things she needed. Four people were already in line at the express lane. "I wonder why they call it express," Jenni muttered to herself. She was tired and in no mood to wait fifteen minutes to buy a half dozen items. Besides, she hated grocery shopping. Myra did most of the shopping and Jenni cooked. That was their trade-off. But Myra was going out with friends tonight, so Jenni had no choice but to pick up the things herself.

Finally she dumped the contents of her basket onto the conveyer belt and watched the checker pass each item over the laser beam. Just as she slid the bread across, the package split open and bread spilled out on the counter.

"Oh, I'm sorry," the woman said. "There must have been a tear in the wrapper."

"I'll just run and get another," Jenni volunteered.

"No, I can have one of the sackers get it for you."

That was fine with Jenni. She was hungry and her feet hurt—a terrible combination, to her way of thinking. The checker got the attention of someone, and they stood waiting for the bread.

"I hope he gets the right one," the woman remarked sarcastically.

"Oh, I'm sure he will," Jenni responded, puzzled by the woman's attitude.

The clerk leaned forward as if she were going to tell Jenni some secret. "You don't understand. Stephen is retarded. He might come back with biscuits!"

Immediately Jenni realized whom she was talking about and started to respond, but Stephen showed up with the loaf of wheat bread and began sacking. Suddenly he looked up and recognized her.

"Jenni! Hi. I've never seen you in here."

"Hello, Stephen. Grocery shopping isn't my favorite sport. That's why you don't see me here."

"Want me to carry these to your car?"

"You bet." Jenni took a step away from the counter, then stopped. "Stephen, would you meet me at the door? I forgot something, but I'll be right there."

"Sure, I'll wait." Stephen walked away and Jenni turned to the checker, who tried not to look at her.

"Excuse me, Dora," Jenni said after she glanced at the woman's nametag. The woman looked toward her, a smirk on her face. "I don't like the way you spoke about my friend Stephen," she began. "You obviously are ill-informed as to the abilities of people who are mentally challenged. Stephen is a very responsible and polite person. You would do well to take a few lessons from him." The woman opened her mouth to speak, but Jenni continued. "And if I ever hear you make another derogatory remark about Stephen or another person who is disabled, I will report you to your manager." Jenni wheeled around and walked out. She had surprised not only the checker and waiting customer, but herself.

She thought about it as she drove to the apartment. *I must be some kind of hypocrite,* she thought to herself. *Here I am defending disabled people when I won't even work with them myself.* She pulled into her parking space and was shocked when Trey jerked the door open.

"Trey! You scared the wits out of me."

"Didn't you see me when you drove in? I waved to you." He took the sack of groceries.

"No," she said absently. "My mind was on other things." Jenni walked up the stairs in front of Trey, digging into her purse for the key to her apartment. "What are you doing here anyway?" She unlocked the door and held it open for Trey. He put the sack of groceries on the kitchen cabinet.

"I'm playing Mr. Fix-it for my aunt."

Jenni glared at him. "You hardly look the type, especially with cut-offs and T-shirt. Aren't you supposed to wear overalls or something?" Trey rolled his eyes upward. Jenni continued to tease him. "What did you do? Change someone's light bulb?"

Trey looked at her in mock dismay. "I'll have you know I fixed someone's toilet for them."

"Oh, yuk!" Jenni put her hands up in defense. "Stay away from me, please!"

"All I did was replace a new flush bar or whatever you call it."

"Whatever you call it? My, aren't we knowledgeable about repairs." She smiled at him.

"Do you mind, Jenni? My ego is plummeting by the minute." He grabbed her by the waist and pulled her toward him.

"Okay, okay, I quit. I won't tease you any more." He let go of her and she backed away from him. "Besides, I don't want to be that close to someone who fixes toilets."

"That's it!" Trey grabbed for her. Jenni screamed and ran through the living room and out the front door. Trey chased her down the veranda, both of them laughing and yelling.

Jenni stopped at the top of the stairs. "I'll bet the neighbors think we're crazy." She leaned back against the railing.

"I'll bet you're right." He put his hands on her shoulders and stared into her eyes. "It just so happens that I'm wild about crazy people."

Jenni chuckled. "Well, you should have been with me at the supermarket. That checker thinks I am one crazy lady." Trey rested one arm around her shoulders and they walked back to the apartment together.

"So what happened at the supermarket?" Trey emptied the sack and Jenni put the items away while she told him about the episode with the checker.

"You told her that?" Trey was beaming.

"Yeah. Can you believe it?" Trey picked her up and swung her around in circles. "What's that for?"

"I told you. I like crazy people." He kissed her lightly on the lips then put her down. "Seriously, I am really proud of you. Not only did you stand up for Stephen, but you took another step toward removing that wall of fear you thought you could never tear down. I told you that you could do it!"

Jenni smiled at Trey's approval. "Thanks. I was really beating up on myself when I came home, thinking I was some kind of hypocrite."

"Don't you dare do that to yourself."

They sat together on the sofa. "But doesn't it seem that way to you?"

"No. You really don't see what happened today, do you, Jenni?" He was turned toward her, arm over the top of the sofa.

"I guess not."

"You defended Stephen, right?"

"Right."

"Why?"

"Well, because. . .because I like Stephen."

"In other words, you defended a friend."

"Yes, but I don't understand what—"

"At that moment, Stephen wasn't some disabled person out there that you were afraid of." Trey was on the edge of the sofa, excitement lighting up his face. "Stephen was your friend, pure and simple." He took hold of her hand. "You did it, Jenni. You broke free of your fear."

Jenni looked at Trey in surprise. "I did, didn't I?" She grabbed him around the neck, then settled in his lap. "I really did it!" Then she thought for a moment. "But what about the next time?"

"Shhh." Trey put his finger to her lips. "We're in the present, not the future. Just thank God for the victory of the moment."

Jenni jumped up from his lap. "Did you hear what you said?"

"What?" Trey looked confused.

"You said, 'Thank God for the victory of the moment.' "

Trey got up, looking troubled. "That's just an expression, Jenni."

"No, it's not." She walked over and put her arms around his waist. "I know you too well."

"Could we get something to eat? I'm starved."

Jenni looked at him with a smile. "Maybe tonight was a victory for both of us." She put her hand to his lips before he could protest. "Come on into the kitchen. I'll fix us a couple of chef salads."

Trey followed. "But I wanted real food. Why don't I run out to McDonald's and—"

"Trey, do you want my company and a salad, or a hamburger and French fries?"

Trey winced. "That's a tough decision." Jenni threw the dishtowel at him. "Okay, okay! Just make sure you put plenty of meat, cheese, eggs, and dressing on mine and none of those sprout things."

nineteen

Jenni entered the music room to the sounds of marching music and children's voices. Karen walked over to greet her.

"Didn't I tell you I'd see you this week? And looks like you're ready to begin," she said, indicating Jenni's leotard and shorts.

"I'm going straight to class from here." Jenni glanced around nervously. "I'm a little scared, Karen. Do you really think I can do it?"

"You'll do fine." Karen gave her a quick hug.

"Then tell me what to do."

"Just let them watch you do something, like a *plié*, or whatever you choose, then have them try it with you. You may need to help them, but they will give it their best."

Jenni kept nodding in agreement while she listened and chewed the inside of her lower lip. "I'm not this nervous at a performance," she confided.

"Just remember what I said. Recognize their worth. And don't think of them as different."

Jenni nodded again and stared at the marching children. "And, Jenni," Karen added, "do what you do when you get onstage. Dance from your heart."

"And glorify God," Jenni added softly with a smile.

"Come on." Karen led her to the center of the room, then turned off the music. "Listen, everyone." All the children turned toward her. "This is Miss Jenni and she's going to help you with your dancing. Now I want you to watch Miss Jenni very carefully and try really hard to do what she tells you. Okay?"

There was a unison of "okays" and jumping up and down. "They're all yours." Karen smiled and walked over to one of the chairs and sat down, gently rubbing her protruding abdomen. Jenni said a silent prayer. *Lord, give me wisdom and patience and the ability to teach these children.*

Stephen walked over to Jenni. "I'm glad you're going to teach."

"Thanks, Stephen. I'm glad you're here to help me."

Stephen beamed a big smile at Jenni's confidence in him.

The children stared at Jenni as she stood in front of them. She felt a little panic rise in her but quickly focused her mind on dancing.

"First of all, everyone take off your shoes." The children scrambled to the floor excitedly, taking off their tennis shoes and giggling. One got up and started jumping up and down. Another sat calmly on the floor, waiting for further instructions.

"Now, let's see. Why don't you line up right here." She motioned to a spot in front of her. "Good. Now spread out." She stretched her arms out straight to her sides. "Give yourself this much room." Some moved, others didn't. She walked over to them and spaced each one of them, giving them room to turn, kick, and bend. "Now, watch me, then you do what I do." A few of the children grinned.

Stephen started the music. Jenni put one arm out to her side and circled one overhead, then lifted one leg gracefully, watching the children the whole time. Some arms went out, some up, some down, and several children hit the floor when they tried to lift their leg like Jenni. All giggled and stood up again. She placed her right foot in front of her, toe pointed, then brought it back. Most children mimicked the movement. After a *demi plié* she turned in a graceful pirouette.

Again, arms went in all directions and some tumbled to the floor when turning circles, yet a few followed some of the movements. Chrissy seemed especially adept.

Kicking proved to be a problem, so Jenni lined them up at the *barre*, then one by one stood beside them and held their hands to keep them balanced as they kicked one leg forward, then the other. Then she leaned each child forward over her arm and helped them kick backward.

The slow music changed to fast, and Jenni switched from ballet to modern dance. She noticed the children adding their own creative movements and following her surprisingly well for a first time. Even Stephen joined the group as they laughed and danced all over the floor.

Karen turned off the music and walked over to the group. "Sorry, guys, but it's time for you to go back to class. I'll see you on Thursday. Stephen, would you take them to their class?" Karen turned to Jenni. "You're a natural with the kids. I've never been able to hold their attention that long."

"I didn't really do anything."

"Yes, you did. You really love dancing, don't you? I mean you really get a sense of fulfillment and enjoyment out of it?"

"Well. . .yes."

"That's what they saw. You see, they love music and dancing as much as you do. That's why you will do well with them—that is, if you want to come back."

"I'll try, if you're sure you want me."

"I want you, believe me. We both want you," she said, patting her pregnant stomach.

"Karen, would you mind not mentioning this to Trey? I'd like to wait and see how I do."

"Okay. But remember, Jenni. All the children want is to have fun and be accepted. And I promise you that you will enjoy it as much as they will once you get to know them."

Jenni turned to leave and found Chrissy beside her, looking up at her. Jenni knelt down beside the little girl. "Chrissy, you did a good job today. I'll be back in two days," she said, holding up two fingers.

Chrissy smiled and grabbed Jenni around the neck in a big hug. Jenni reluctantly put her arm around the child and hugged her. She prayed silently, *Lord, help me to love these children, especially this little girl that You keep bringing into my life.*

By the end of the second week Jenni was beginning to really enjoy the children. She rummaged through the wardrobe department and picked out discarded costumes and accessories to take with her to the school. Mrs. Thatcher approved of her working with the children as long as it didn't interfere with her work at the theater.

As she walked into the music room with the big box, she watched the expectant expressions on the children's faces. She put the box on the floor in the middle of the room. Everyone gathered around her, quieter than she had ever seen them.

"Want to see what's in the box?" They all nodded eagerly and gathered around the box as Jenni pulled out bright-colored scarves, over-used tutus, hats, headpieces, and more. The children laughed as they swapped costumes and wrapped scarves completely around their little bodies. Jenni put tutus on the girls and pinned them to fit.

"Come over to the mirror and look at yourselves." They followed her to the *barre* in front of the mirrored wall. Each child acted out some thought as to what he or she looked like, giggling at each other's costumes. Patrick jumped up and down, enjoying the hat flopping forward over his face. Emily ran around the room, her bright gold scarf flowing behind her. Chrissy stared into the mirror without moving. Jenni walked over to her and fluffed the white net of Chrissy's tutu. "It's a ballerina's skirt," she said, kneeling down beside Chrissy. "Let me show you." Jenni took another tutu out of the box and slipped it over her own shorts and joined Chrissy. "Now, we're twins." Chrissy smiled and hugged Jenni.

"This is what a ballerina does." Jenni came up on her toes and did a *pirouette*, then a *révérence*. Chrissy watched, then grabbed Jenni as she bowed forward on the reverence. They both fell to the floor and the rest of the children joined them. Jenni tickled a few and they threw themselves into her lap and around her neck.

Karen walked over to the group, and Jenni looked up at her

from the floor. "I think I lost control of this class," she said, nearly choking from Patrick's grip around her neck. They both laughed.

"Okay, guys," Karen clapped her hands for attention. "Put the costumes away and go to class with Stephen. They all jumped up and ran to the box, jerking off all the paraphernalia. Jenni slipped out of the tutu and threw it into the box and closed the lid.

"Thanks, Jenni. The kids had a ball."

"It's just a bunch of stuff that's not being used anymore, but I thought they might have some fun with it." She carried the box to the door and waited for Karen to open it.

"You're having fun, aren't you, Jenni?"

"It shows?" Jenni smiled at Karen.

"Yes! A lot! But I dare not say I told you so." They both laughed and Jenni hurried to her car and drove to the studio.

Pinning her hair into a bun, Jenni hurried to class.

"Jenni." Mrs. Thatcher called to her. "There's a young man waiting to see you. He's in the lobby."

Jenni walked toward the lobby wondering why Mrs. Thatcher didn't just say Trey was waiting. Everyone at the theater knew him by now. *He must be on his way back to school from his homebound student,* she thought. Then she saw a dark-haired man standing by the door, looking outside. He turned toward her.

"Doug!" she exclaimed in disbelief. Before she had taken a step toward him, he grabbed her and whirled her around with a hug. "What. . .what are you doing here?" she asked when he finally put her down.

Doug didn't answer right away but kept his arms around her, looking at her from glistening brown eyes.

Jenni pulled away a little and Doug loosened his hold, keeping one arm around her waist. "I can't believe you're here."

"Your letters made Florida sound so exciting, I decided to take a few days off and see for myself."

"It's great to see you, but why didn't you let me know you were coming?"

"I wanted to surprise you."

"You certainly did that. Have you already found a place to stay? When did you get here?"

"Wait, wait," he laughed. "One question at a time."

"I'm sorry. You know me."

"I hope so," he said, looking directly at Jenni. She dropped her gaze toward the floor. Doug continued his conversation as if he didn't notice.

"I rented a car at the airport and came straight here. But it looks like you're pretty busy right now."

"Right. I have class now and rehearsal until late afternoon. I'm really sorry." Jenni started to walk slowly across the lobby, Doug's arm still around her.

"No problem. I'd like to find a place to stay and look around Cocoa Beach. Why don't we have dinner tonight?"

Jenni hesitated. She was expecting Trey.

"Of course, if you have other plans." Doug looked at her quizzically.

"No! No. Dinner would be great," she quickly interjected, wondering how she would explain this to Trey. "It just might need to be late."

"That's fine."

"Let me tell you how to get to my apartment."

Doug took a small notepad and pen from his pocket, and Jenni thought how typical this was of Doug. She wrote her address and drew a little map. "It's easy to find."

"I think I can manage. I'll see you around. . .what? Eight okay?"

"Eight would be perfect."

Jenni's thoughts were troubled all afternoon. How was she going to explain Doug's presence to Trey? She wondered if he would be jealous or understanding. She even wondered which way she actually wanted him to react. Certainly she wanted his understanding, but she hoped he would voice some displeasure over Doug's presence, showing that she placed strongly in his heart.

And what about Doug? How was she going to tell him she was in love with another man, especially someone she had only met this summer? Doug would never understand.

She and her partner worked on their *pas de deux* most of the afternoon, and she finished earlier than she had planned.

At home she showered and dressed in comfortable cutoffs and oversized shirt. Turning on the ceiling fan, she sat down on the sofa with a cup of hot tea. She would relax a few minutes, then call Trey. A knock at the door startled her.

"Trey! What. . .what are you doing here?"

"Are you going to ask me in?"

Jenni stepped away from the door. "Of course, but I thought—"

"I know. I'm not supposed to be here until tonight, but something came up. I have to go to a meeting in Orlando for speech pathologists. I forgot about it until I was at school, so I thought I would just run by and tell you rather than call. This way I still get to see you."

"Oh, that's fine."

"Well, you could act a little disappointed," Trey said, circling his arms around Jenni while she still held the cup of tea.

"Trey!" She grabbed the cup as it jiggled on the saucer.

"Well, put it down! What's wrong with you? You seem jumpy."

Jenni pulled away. "Nothing's wrong. I just got home from rehearsal and I'm tired." She put the cup of tea on the table.

She realized now was the time to tell Trey about Doug but decided she should wait since he was going out of town. *After all,* she reasoned, *Doug will probably leave tomorrow once I tell him about Trey.*

"Jenni, are you sure you feel well?"

"I'm fine. Why do you ask?"

"I'm not sure. You just seem. . .distant. Just tired, I guess."

"I am. Today was hectic."

Trey put his arms around her and kissed her lightly on the forehead. "Maybe you're working too hard."

Jenni laid her head against his chest. "No, I'm not. You're a worrier, like my mother."

Trey pushed her slightly away from him. "Hey, wait. I'm not sure that's much of a compliment."

"Of course it is. I love my mother very much." Jenni stopped short, wondering how he would take the comment.

"Does that mean you love me very much, too?" Trey asked, looking at her with sky blue eyes.

She wanted to say, *Yes, yes, with my whole heart I love you*, yet she could only look at him and say nothing.

Trey's mouth came down softly on hers, then pressed harder as he pulled her to him. Jenni circled her arms around him, lacing her fingers through his hair. Her heart pounded with the passion of their kiss. The sweet, spicy smell of his cologne only enhanced her desires as his lips met hers again. Suddenly Jenni pushed away from him.

"I think you'd better go." She put her hand to her quivering lips.

"I know. But I don't want to leave."

"Trey," Jenni looked at him pleadingly.

Trey tilted her chin up with his hand. "Don't worry, I'm going. But we need to talk."

"Not right now." Jenni turned away. She couldn't possibly talk intelligently right now.

Trey turned her back to face him. "I don't mean right now, but soon."

Jenni circled her arms around his waist and put her face against his chest. She felt his hand stroke her hair.

"Jenni, do you have any idea how much I love—"

She quickly put her hand up to his lips. "Not now. Please, not right now." She had waited so long to hear "I love you." But she couldn't bear hearing those words right before going out with Doug.

twenty

"If the food matches the atmosphere, this shrimp scampi should be spectacular," Doug said. The pier restaurant was elegantly furnished. Burgundy tablecloths covered tables set with crystal water goblets and linen napkins.

"It is lovely, isn't it? And I enjoy the live piano music."

Doug reached over and took Jenni's hand. "What I like most is being here with you. This has been the longest summer of my entire life."

Jenni tried to keep light conversation going throughout the dinner. "Well, tell me about everyone back home. How about church? Does Mrs. Wallace still sing in the choir?"

"Yep. And still a little off-key," Doug said with a smile. "She asks about you every Sunday."

"How old is she? She's got to be in her seventies, don't you think?"

"Wrong! She celebrated her eighty-fifth birthday last month. The whole church was invited. Oh, and you know that older man who always sits on the very end of the front row? I've forgotten his name. I think the two of them may have a little romance brewing. I actually saw him wink at Mrs. Wallace one Sunday morning." They both laughed.

"The church I attend here is much smaller. The main thing I miss is the wonderful music we had with our large choir."

"The main thing I miss is you."

Jenni couldn't bring herself to look at Doug. He was so happy. She had to keep reminding herself what she had to do. It wasn't that she didn't want to tell him about Trey, she just didn't like hurting him in the process. She had decided that it would be easier to talk at the apartment over a cup of coffee rather than at the restaurant. She chided herself again for not telling Doug about Trey through a letter or phone call.

"How's Mother?" she asked, finally looking at Doug. "I really miss her. I guess that sounds childish coming from a twenty-four-year-old, doesn't it?"

"No. I know how close the two of you are."

Jenni smiled. "I can hardly wait to see her."

Doug reached across the table and took hold of her hand. "That's what I was hoping you would say. Come back with me, Jenni. That's the reason I came."

Jenni looked at Doug with disbelief.

"I want to marry you, Jenni. Don't you know that?"

"Doug. . ."

"Please come home with me."

Jenni pulled her hand away. "Do you expect me to leave the theater—walk out, just like that?"

"Yes."

"How could you ask me to do something like that? I made a commitment for the summer."

"And what if you didn't have that commitment? Then would you come home with me?"

"What's that supposed to mean?"

"I guess I'm asking if you're seeing someone here."

The question surprised Jenni. She didn't answer. She didn't want to discuss this right now.

"I thought so," Doug said quietly.

Jenni tried to head off the conversation. "Why don't we skip dessert and go to my apartment for coffee? We can talk there."

Doug pushed his plate away and looked across the table at Jenni. "Why can't we talk here?"

"I just think it would be more comfortable at the apartment." Jenni lowered her gaze, not wanting to look at Doug.

"Why didn't you tell me, Jenni?"

She stared at a water spot on the tablecloth for a moment, then looked up at Doug. "I don't know. I'm sorry. I should have told you."

"So. . ." Doug shook his head. "So," he began again. "What's his name?" He folded his arms on the table in front of him and looked at Jenni without expression.

"I don't think that's important."

"No, I suppose not." Doug picked up the saltshaker and tapped it on the table while they sat in silence.

"I suppose he's a tall blond lifeguard or water-skiing instructor, with lots of muscle and little brains," he said, clutching the small glass bottle in his hand.

Jenni knew Doug's sarcasm was covering the hurt he felt. She wished she could make it easier for both of them. "He is tall and blond, but he's a speech pathologist, not a lifeguard."

"I'm sorry. You didn't deserve that remark." Doug meticulously put the saltshaker back in its place.

"Doug, I wanted to tell you about Trey, but I just didn't know how. I didn't want to hurt you."

"So when did you plan on telling me, Jenni?" He gave her a questioning look. "At the end of the summer? No, wait." He held up one hand. "Let me guess. You're not coming home."

"I agree I should have written. I'm sorry."

Doug let out a quiet chuckle. "I thought we had a future together, Jenni. I love you and want you to be my wife. You know that."

Jenni stiffened a little. "Yes, I know. But I never made any promises, Doug."

Doug hesitated for only a moment. "So what do you expect me to do? Book a flight tomorrow so I don't inconvenience you too much?" Doug was raising his voice and the couple at the table next to them glanced in their direction.

"Doug, please don't act this way."

"What do you expect me to do?"

"I don't know."

"I come all the way from Oklahoma to find you're crazy about some *speech pathologist* and you ask me not to act like this!"

"I didn't ask you to come!"

"That's true, you didn't." Doug was silent for a few moments. "I think we'd better go."

Neither of them spoke on the short drive to the apartment.

"Would you like to come in for a cup of coffee?" Jenni asked when they arrived, not knowing what else to do.

"No." Doug stared out the car window.

"Doug. . .I don't know what to say."

"Well, that makes two of us." He got out of the car and opened her door.

"You don't need to walk me upstairs."

"Why? Is he waiting for you?"

Anger and hurt burned inside of Jenni. Not trusting herself to speak, she quickly turned and walked to the stairs. Doug ran after her and caught hold of her arm.

"I'm sorry, Jenni. Could I call you in the morning? I just can't talk right now."

"I have class tomorrow morning and rehearsal during the afternoon."

"Okay." Doug stuffed his hands in his pockets and took a couple of deep breaths to calm himself. "So when would be a good time for you, Jenni?"

She noted the sarcasm in his voice. "There is no good time, Doug. I don't want to argue any more."

"You mean you want me to just turn around and go home and act like this never happened?"

"No, I'm not saying that." Jenni paused and let out a long sigh. "I don't have to be at class until ten-thirty. You could come by about eight if you want."

Doug nodded. "I'll be here." He left Jenni standing at the bottom of the stairs and walked back to the driver's side of the car and left.

Jenni watched him drive away, then walked up the stairs alone, wishing Trey really were waiting inside for her.

❧

The morning sun was already bright as Jenni walked out onto the veranda. This was just one more thing she loved about

Florida. When she was feeling low, she had only to step outside and immediately she felt better. Even the frequent afternoon rain showers were quickly replaced by sunshine.

She glanced toward the parking lot, watching for Doug. He had called to tell her he was on his way over. She hoped they could talk without hurting each other. She would like to be friends. She realized now that all she had ever wanted from Doug was friendship. His rental car pulled into the parking area and Jenni walked to the stairs. He was dressed in khaki walking shorts, white knit shirt, and straw hat. He saw her at the top of the stairs and waved.

"Do I look like a native?" he asked when he reached the top of the stairs, hands stuffed in his pockets.

"You look fine," Jenni said with a smile. "Come on in."

"This is nice," Doug said, looking around the small living room.

"Come on into the kitchen." Jenni had plates of fresh fruit, juice, and rolls.

"You shouldn't have gone to such trouble."

"It was no trouble. Sit down and I'll pour coffee."

"I'm sorry I lost my temper last night, Jenni." Doug pulled out a chair and sat down at the small table.

"Maybe we shouldn't talk about it anymore." She poured coffee then sat down across from Doug.

Doug took a drink of his coffee and ate a few grapes from his plate. Jenni sipped on orange juice.

"Sorry I don't have watermelon. I know how much you like it," Jenni said to cover the silence.

"Oh, no, this is great. Cantaloupe, and what's this? Honeydew melon?"

Jenni nodded.

"I'm not hard to please when it comes to food. Not that this isn't exceptional," he quickly added.

Jenni laughed. "It's okay, Doug. You don't have to charm me. I. . .hope we can still be friends." She paused. "I'm really sorry for not telling you about Trey. You shouldn't have found out this way." Doug was silent, so Jenni continued. "I wanted to tell you, I really did. I. . .I just didn't know how."

Doug pushed his plate away from him and leaned back in his chair. "I stayed up most of the night thinking," Doug said. "About three o'clock this morning I realized something. You've never loved me, Jenni." Jenni stared at the glass of juice in her hands. She didn't want to look at Doug. She didn't want to see the pain in his eyes. "I wanted you to love me," Doug added.

"Doug—" Jenni looked across the table, but Doug put up a hand to stop her comment and continued.

"Wait. I have something to say. You owe me this."

Jenni nodded her agreement.

"As I said, I wanted you to love me and I tried everything I knew to make it happen. That's why I was so mad last night. In fact, I was angrier at myself than at you. I guess I knew when you boarded that plane in Oklahoma City that you were walking away from me forever and I was angry that I didn't stop you."

"Doug, you couldn't have stopped me," Jenni said gently.

"I know." Doug let a brief smile cross his face. He got up and poured himself another cup of coffee and walked over to the window. "It's hard to let go of a dream, Jenni. You've talked of your dream of being a ballerina in a metropolitan ballet, so you would know about such things." She turned in her chair to see him staring out the window. He turned and looked at her. "You were my dream, Jenni."

She didn't want to hear this. She wished he would just get mad and walk out like he did last night. That would be easier. "Doug, I wanted to love you the way you loved me. I tried, but. . ."

Doug set his cup on the table and pulled a chair up beside her. "I know that, Jenni, and I even love you for doing that. I admit I didn't act like it last night, but after I thought about it and prayed most of the night, God showed me something very special."

Jenni looked up in surprise.

Doug took one of her hands in his. "I finally realized that you had always loved me with a very special love and I was trying to change it into something it was never meant to be. You were offering me friendship—a real, loving friendship—and I was throwing it back in your face because I wanted something different."

Jenni felt tears brim her eyes and spill down her cheeks. Doug reached up and wiped them away.

"I want that love, Jenni," he almost whispered. "More than anything. I want that special love you offer in just being my friend."

Jenni squeezed Doug's hand, unable to speak. He took her face between his hands and looked into her eyes. "I love you, Jenni, and I think it's okay. And maybe one day I will love someone the way you love Trey. And when I do, I know she will love me in the same way."

Jenni grabbed Doug around the neck and hugged him tightly, letting tears drop onto his shirt. She leaned back, wiped her cheeks with her hands, and looked at him. "You are one of the sweetest men I know."

"And who is the other one?" he asked with a smile.

She turned her face away.

"No, I'm serious," Doug said, standing up. "Let's go into the living room, and you can tell me about your speech pathologist. I don't know that I've ever met one." Doug sat on the sofa and Jenni sat in a chair adjacent to him. She looked at him questioningly.

"Are you sure you really want to hear about Trey?"

"I'm positive." Doug sat back, sipping his coffee.

"Well, he's not like most speech pathologists," Jenni began. "He teaches developmentally disabled children. And you should see them, Doug." She leaned forward in her chair. "I'm teaching them to dance. That's where I was before class yesterday. Chrissy is really good. She doesn't speak, but she dances beautifully and has such potential. She uses sign language and always hugs me and signs 'I love you' when I leave. And Patrick is such a clown. There are five of them. I never thought I could do it, but I'm having so much fun." Suddenly Jenni stopped, realizing she was rambling on about the children.

Doug was smiling at her. "I've never seen you like this."

"Like what?"

"So. . .so exuberant, excited. There's just a sparkle about you. Yet I can't imagine you teaching disabled children."

"I know. I was so scared at first. But God has really changed my life. And you're right, Doug. I am happy." She stopped, then added quietly, "I'm very happy."

Doug put his coffee on the table beside him and reached for Jenni's hand. "That's all I need to know."

They spent the next half-hour talking about friends and old times in Oklahoma City. Jenni glanced at the clock. "Oh, Doug, I hate to rush you off, but I've got to get to class."

"That's okay. I need to call the airport and see if I can change my flight."

"You're not leaving already?"

"I think it's best. You're busy and I've found out what I need to know." Doug clasped his hands in front of him, leaning forward on the sofa.

"I really am sorry, Doug. I never wanted to hurt you."

"I know that, Jenni. Remember, we've been friends a long time. I know you well enough to understand your motives, or lack of motives, I should say." Jenni smiled. Doug stood up and reached down for her hand. "Come on. Walk an old friend to the door."

Jenni took his hand. "I'll do better than that. I'll even walk you to the stairs." They both laughed, and Jenni was certain she saw a smile of true friendship from Doug.

"Tell Mother hello for me and that I miss her but I'll be home soon."

"Are you sure about that?" Doug glanced at her as they walked along the veranda.

"Sure about what?"

"That you will be going home." They stopped at the top of the stairs, and Jenni leaned back against the railing. "I have a feeling someone is going to try to keep you in Florida as hard as I tried to keep you in Oklahoma. But I think he's going to succeed."

"Just give her my love."

"That I will do." Doug leaned forward and kissed her tenderly on the lips. "Good-bye, Jenni."

"Well, what have we here?" Jenni suddenly turned at the sound of the familiar voice. "Trey! Wh–what are you doing here?"

Trey stood at the top of the stairs, feet apart, hands on his hips, staring at Jenni. "Well, from the looks of things I'd say I'm interrupting." He looked from Jenni to Doug.

"No! No, you're not." Jenni was confused. She looked at Doug, wondering what she should do and why she couldn't think.

Doug broke the silence. "I'm Doug Williams, a friend of Jenni's." Doug extended his hand. Trey glared at him and made no attempt to accept the handshake.

"Trey, this is Doug." Jenni was finally getting her senses about her.

"He just said that and I don't really care who he is." Jenni could see the anger burning in Trey's eyes. How could she explain this quickly and simply?

"I think I'd better go." Doug took a step toward the stairs.

"No, I'll go," Trey said, cutting a look at Jenni. "Sorry for the interruption." He turned and started down the stairs, taking the steps two at a time.

"Trey, wait!" She stood at the top of the steps, unable to move, her gaze fixed on his car as he peeled out of the parking area.

twenty-one

"You've got to eat," Myra scolded during lunch break. Jenni nibbled on a bran muffin but didn't respond.

"Come on, Jenni. You couldn't help what happened."

"Of course I could." Jenni looked up at Myra. "I should have told Trey that Doug was here. I don't blame him for getting angry." She put the muffin on her plate and shoved it away. "What am I going to do?"

Myra wadded her paper napkin and put it on the plate in front of her. "You know that Trey has a tendency to. . .ummm, let's see. How should I put it? He tends to overreact at times, wouldn't you say?"

"Is that a kind way of saying he has a terrible temper?" A weak smile crossed Jenni's face.

"Yeah, that's exactly what I'm saying. Give him awhile to cool off, then you can work things out. In fact, he will probably be here tonight. You know he doesn't miss a Friday night performance."

"I don't know." Jenni pursed her lips and shook her head. "He was more than angry." She thought back for a moment. "I think he was really hurt." Jenni propped her elbows on the table and leaned her forehead on her clasped hands. "How could I have made such a mess of things?" Her voice rose in anger at herself.

"Stop it, Jenni!" Myra stood up. "That's enough." She gathered their disposable lunch containers and pitched them in the trash. "What's done is done. You don't need blame or pity. You and Trey will work things out. Now let's get to rehearsal." Jenni followed compliantly, hoping she was right.

❧

Myra came offstage from her dance variation and Jenni hurried over to her. "Did you see Trey in the audience?"

"No. But that doesn't mean he's not here. You can't see much under those lights. You know that."

"But there are no flowers. He always sends flowers to my dressing room on Friday nights." Tears pricked the back of her eyes, threatening to surface. Jenni tilted her head backwards and blinked them back. "Oh, Myra, what am I going to do?"

"You're going to go out there and dance better than you've ever danced before."

"But what if he doesn't come tonight?"

"Then I guess you'll see him tomorrow. Now stop worrying and get ready for your *pas de deux*. Here, let me fix your flower." Myra reached up and straightened the flower in Jenni's hair. "There. You look great."

"Thanks, Myra." Jenni took deep breaths and did foot stretches while she waited. Myra was right. She had work to do and her problems with Trey would have to wait until the next day. But something in her heart told her things would be no different when the morning came.

❧

Early Saturday morning Jenni called Trey's house but got his answering machine. She left a message. An hour passed and she left four more messages, one every fifteen minutes. She tried one last time. "This is Trey Maddox. Please leave your name and phone number and I'll return your call."

"No, you won't!" Jenni slammed the receiver down and grabbed her purse. "Myra, I'll be gone for a while," she called over her shoulder. She drove straight to Trey's house and found him in the yard working on the old white van. He was dressed in oily, grimy clothes, his blond hair smudged with grease, and his blue eyes gave no indication that he was happy to see her.

She walked over to the van. "Can we talk?"

"I don't think there is anything to talk about," Trey said without interrupting his work.

"I want to explain."

"I don't think that's necessary." He leaned farther under the hood while tightening something with a wrench, then stood up straight, wiping perspiration from his face on the sleeve of his shirt.

Jenni was perturbed at his indifference. "I just want to explain what happened."

"No, thanks. Obviously I misunderstood our relationship." He slammed the hood of the van down and jerked a rag from his back pocket and wiped his hands.

"Why do you say that?"

"Quit acting so naive, Jenni. It's not appealing." He started to walk away.

"Trey!" Jenni called. "It wasn't what it seemed." Trey turned toward her. "That was Doug."

"I know it was Doug." He glared at her. "You both told me that, remember?" He walked toward the house.

"But you don't know who Doug is. He's my friend from Oklahoma. The one I told you about."

Trey stopped and walked back to her. "Oh, *that* Doug! The one you left?" He was face-to-face with her.

"Yes."

"The one you didn't love? The one you were never going back to?"

"Well. . .yes. But it's not what you think. Just let me explain."

"Please, spare me."

"But he's gone."

"Oh, so now we pick up where we left off. Is that it, Jenni? No thanks."

"Trey, listen to me. It's you I love, not Doug."

"Well, it sure didn't seem that way the other day." His gaze never left Jenni's face.

"I know, and I'm trying to explain it."

Trey's expression softened. "Why didn't you tell me he was coming?"

"I didn't know. He just showed up. Then I decided it would

be best to tell you after you got back from Orlando."

Trey's anger flashed again. "You mean you were planning to go out with that guy when I was at the apartment?"

Jenni was close to tears. She was doing a terrible job of explaining Doug's presence. "Well. . .yes. . .I mean. . .I knew he was here. We—"

"Never mind, Jenni. I've heard enough."

"I didn't plan it, Trey."

"Yeah, well, I didn't plan to fall in love with you, either. Seems we both made a big mistake." He wheeled around and walked toward the house.

"Trey! Don't walk away!"

"Go home, Jenni," Trey called over his shoulder. "Doug is probably waiting." He walked into the house, slamming the screen door.

Jenni stood in the middle of the yard, tears slipping down her cheeks. Finally she walked to her car and sat for a few minutes, staring blindly at Trey's house. "But I didn't know he was coming," she whispered, oblivious to the tears that wet her cheeks. "And I didn't know you loved me that much." She covered her face with her hands and shook with sobs.

twenty-two

Except for the time she spent at the theater and with the children at school, time seemed to drag by. Jenni hadn't seen Trey, nor had she tried to get in touch with him any further. Once she thought she saw him in the audience at a performance, but he didn't come backstage or send flowers.

In less than two weeks she would be leaving everything she had come to love over these last three months. The summer position at the theater would be finished. The relationship with Trey was already over. Still, she didn't want to go home. But what else could she do?

Struggling to find peace, Jenni got up early Saturday morning, grabbed her portable cassette player and tapes, and drove to the beach. At home when she was troubled she had always gone to the field behind their house, played her favorite tape, and danced. There among the trees and wildflowers she could abandon all desires to please an audience and meditate on the words of the praise songs she loved to play. No worry about getting a position just right, or perfect timing with her partner. She could dance from her heart.

She found an area of beach in the park reserve and walked to the water's edge to watch the sun spread its colors over the water. Trey was probably standing on this same beach, watching this same sunrise, just a few miles up the shoreline. She would like to be watching it with him. She would like to spend a lifetime watching sunrises with him, but she wanted something else even more. She turned on the tape player and slipped off her shoes. The morning sand felt cool against her bare feet.

As the music began, Jenni lifted her arms toward heaven and moved slowly and gracefully. Sounds of stringed instruments and the background of the ocean surf wafted through the air. There were no words on the instrumental, but Jenni knew the lyrics by heart. She sang Psalm 42 silently as she danced. "As the deer pants for streams of water, so my soul pants for you, O God."

This was Jenni's worship. Like David in the Psalms, she danced before the Lord in her joy of His love. It provided the surrender she needed to open herself completely to His will.

When the song ended, Jenni knelt in the sand and surrendered every part of her life to God. She gave Him her dance, her love for Trey, her work with the children, everything. Then she walked along the water's edge. The sun warmed her while cool water washed over her feet and ankles, giving her a sense of God's love washing over her heart and soul. She had finally found peace.

She drove back to the apartment, relaxed and refreshed. Myra had just gotten up. "Where have you been this early in the morning?"

"To the beach."

"The beach! I had hoped you would say the donut shop." She put a kettle of water on the range to boil.

"Myra, you know you don't need donuts."

"I know, but they're my weakness. You know that."

"Yes, I do." She walked up to her friend and produced a sack from behind her back. "I figured we could splurge today. Sort of celebrate."

Myra squealed. "Oh, Jenni, thank you." Then she looked at her with a puzzled expression. "But what are we celebrating?" She poured tea into delicate china cups while holding a chocolate donut in the other hand.

Jenni sat down at the little table and sipped the hot tea. "You know how upset I've been lately?"

"Boy, do I!" Myra said between bites.

"Well, I'm not anymore."

"Why? Did you talk with Trey?"

"No, I've talked with God."

"What do you mean?"

"Well, at home, when I felt lonely or extremely troubled, I would go to the field behind our house and dance."

"You're kidding." Myra reached for her second donut.

"No, I'm not. I would take my cassette player and tapes and dance until I was exhausted or until I felt an answer to my problem. It seems to be the way God speaks to me."

Myra listened carefully.

Jenni put her teacup on the saucer and pushed it slightly away from her. She propped her elbows on the table and rested her chin on one hand. "That's what I did this morning. I danced alone on the beach and listened for God to speak to me."

"You do seem different. I've been worried about you."

"I know. I couldn't ask for a better friend." She reached over and patted Myra's hand. "But I'm going to be okay." Jenni got up and started to walk off, but Myra grabbed her arm.

"Wait a minute. You sit down and tell me what you're going to do."

Jenni laughed. "Yes, Mother." She sat back down across from Myra. "It's really quite simple. I guess I'll be leaving Florida."

"That's it?"

"That's it," Jenni said with a smile.

"But you love it here. What about the theater and Trey? Oh, and the kids. What about the kids?"

"I love all those things, and I'll miss every one of them."

"Then why are you leaving?"

Jenni looked directly at Myra. "Because I love God even more than I love Florida, dancing, or even Trey. I have to do what He tells me to do. I want to do it."

"That's why you went to the beach?"

"Yes. That's what I had to find out this morning. I needed to give my will over to Him. I had been fighting too long and I needed to find peace."

"So where are you going?"

"Back home."

"Do you think you and Doug will get back together?"

"No, that's over. Doug is a fine Christian man and will be a wonderful husband for someone. But he's not God's choice for me. I suspected that before I left Oklahoma, but now I know for certain."

"But, Jenni, are you sure God wants you to leave?"

"No. I guess that's the real problem. But I want to be open to what He wants for me, and face it, Myra, it doesn't seem to be Florida. I just couldn't stay here, feeling the way I do about Trey."

"I just hate for you to leave."

Both sat silently for a while, and Jenni saw tears slip down Myra's cheeks.

"Myra, are you crying?"

"I'm sorry. I promised myself I wouldn't do this," she said, wiping her eyes and cheeks with her napkin. "I just know how much you love Trey, and I think he's such a. . .a rotten jerk."

"A rotten jerk?" Jenni had to laugh.

"So my vocabulary failed me." Myra laughed, too. "It was the best I could come up with at the moment. I just can't stand seeing you hurt."

Jenni got up and hugged Myra. "You're a great friend. Now let's quit crying and do something. We both have the day off and it's the last one we'll have together, so let's go to Orlando and shop."

Myra's eyes lit up. "Shopping and donuts, both in the same day. I must be in heaven."

❧

On Sunday afternoon Jenni saw Trey helping his aunt with some gardening. She watched him from the window, wishing she could take him a glass of iced tea and just sit close to him and talk, but she did neither. She had done all she could. The rest was up to Trey. She was sorry she hadn't told him about Doug's being in town. She was also sorry she had hurt him, but she had made apologies and explanations. If Trey couldn't accept that, then it was best their relationship ended.

As much as she loved him, she could not spend her life with someone who walked out on problems and turned his back on God. She had hoped to help Trey over his bitterness toward God and thought she had seen progress, but now it seemed she had only given him one more reason to hold on to his bitterness.

On Sunday evening Jenni attended another performance of Ballet Shekinah. She went alone, thankful for the time to think and pray during the forty-five-minute drive to Orlando.

She sat transfixed during the performance. In the past, if she attended a ballet performance, she always noted the choreography, timing between partners, and different dance variations, wondering how she would do that same combination.

But tonight she did none of that. She let the praise songs and the worshipful movements of each dancer invade her heart. Suddenly they were performing the number that Jenni had watched at their rehearsal, praising the names of God. The words of the music brought the same surrender to her heart that she felt at the beach. As the dance climaxed, the performers leaped across the stage in strong *grands jetés* as the names of God resonated through the auditorium. Jenni held her breath and tears burned beneath the surface as she watched and listened. *Jehovah-Shammah, Jehovah-Ropheh, Jehovah-Raah, Jehovah-Jireh. . .*

"Oh, I want to do that," she whispered under her breath. The emotion inside nearly choked her. *Lord, I want to dance for You,* she prayed silently. *I don't care where You send me, just let me glorify You.*

After the performance Jenni made her way backstage and found Lyn. "That was the most beautiful dance I have ever seen."

"Well, thank you, Jenni. I'm so glad to see you again and glad you enjoyed the performance."

"It's even better than I remembered. I. . .I'm speechless, I guess." They both laughed. "Honestly, I have never seen anything like it. It was just. . .exquisite."

Lyn smiled. "Thanks. It always means a lot to me when another performer compliments my dance, especially one with your talent." Lyn held her hand up to prevent Jenni's protest. "Huh-uh. I know talent when I see it. Come sit with me while I take off my makeup and tell me how things are going with you."

"I don't want to take up your time." Jenni felt a little awkward. Maybe she shouldn't have come backstage. "I just wanted to say hello and tell you how much I enjoyed the performance. You're busy."

"Nonsense. I've got lots of time. Now come sit with me. I want to know what was so special for you tonight."

While Lyn took off her makeup, Jenni told her how she felt while watching the performance. "I've been dancing all my life, but I never felt what I felt tonight. Does that make any sense?"

Lyn glanced at her, holding a tissue in her hand. "Perfect sense. Remember, you're talking to someone who has been where you are. What do you think it means, Jenni?" She continued wiping makeup from her face.

"I'm not sure. But I felt so close to the Lord, just like I do when I dance alone to my praise tapes, when I'm dancing for no one except God. No audience approval, no fear of getting some movement absolutely perfect or being in unison with my partner. Just worshipping and praising the Lord. But I'm not sure I would feel that way onstage," she quickly added.

"Do you think God could be speaking to you?" Lyn turned toward Jenni.

"Meaning what?"

"Well, let me ask you this. How is your dream holding up?"

"You mean to make it to the metropolitan ballet?"

"Right." Lyn had finished removing her makeup and was giving Jenni her full attention.

"It doesn't seem so important anymore." Jenni told her

about the disagreement with Trey and surrendering her will at the beach.

"I'm sorry about the problem with Trey, but sometimes God works in people's hearts in unusual ways. Sounds like Trey is fighting God, not you."

"I thought about that and I think it's probably true, but I can't help him with that."

"I'm glad you recognize that. But don't lose faith."

Jenni only smiled but didn't respond.

"But what about you?" Lyn reached out and took hold of Jenni's hand.

Jenni was silent for a moment. "There has been so much happening in my life these last few weeks. Some good, some. . ." Her voice trailed off and she felt tears beginning to surface. Lyn squeezed her hand. Jenni reached up and wiped away a tear that escaped and trickled down her cheek. Lyn handed her a tissue. "But it's funny, though," Jenni went on. "I have more peace now than I have had all summer. I'm not extremely happy," she said with a low chuckle, "but I have peace. And while I watched that last dance, all I could do was ask God to let me dance for Him. I don't care if it's in Oklahoma or where, I just want to dance for the Lord. That's my greatest desire right now. Just praising God."

Lyn let out a big "whoopee" and jumped up from her chair. "Do you think you're ready to join us?"

"What?" Jenni looked at her with astonishment.

"I told you that I've watched you perform. I know you're good and now I know your greatest desire is to glorify God with your gift of dance. That's what I was waiting to see."

"I. . .I don't know what to say. It's an honor and part of me wants to grab the opportunity before I wake up and find it's a dream," Jenni said, and Lyn smiled knowingly. "But I don't know if I should stay in Florida, feeling the way I do about Trey. Maybe I need some distance. . .to heal. You know what I mean?"

Lyn squatted down in front of Jenni and took her hand.

"And maybe you need to let the Lord quiet that part of your spirit, too. You don't have to give me an answer right now. Take some time and pray about it. In fact, let's you and I pray about it right now."

Lyn prayed for peace, wisdom, and direction for Jenni. "Now, go home and let God speak to you. Call me when you're ready."

Jenni and Lyn stood up. "Thank you so much." Jenni hugged Lyn and drove back to Cocoa Beach, still amazed at the feelings inside her. What had happened to her big dream to be a classical ballerina in New York City? It was gone. Now her greatest desire was to glorify God, and she hoped that could be done with Ballet Shekinah. But how? How could she look at another sunrise over the ocean and not think of Trey? What if she ran into him somewhere and the pain returned?

Oh, God, she prayed as she drove through the darkness. *I truly want to do Your will. Give me the wisdom to discern what it is and the courage to follow, wherever You lead me.*

twenty-three

Today was Jenni's last day to teach the children. She was both excited and melancholy. She had actually enjoyed the weeks she had worked with them and would miss them. She thought about the day she brought hats and scarves from the theater's wardrobe and how the children dressed up in costumes and giggled continuously. Then just last week she was showing them a movement and turned around to find them turning somersaults. Jenni smiled. Where were those stoic children she had expected? These kids overflowed with expression.

Of course her star pupil was Chrissy, with her delicate little body and "almost" graceful dance steps. Chrissy would nearly burst with giggles and sign language each time Jenni met with them. Jenni tried to spend extra time with her because she was so adept at learning the dance techniques. God had answered her prayer. She had genuinely fallen in love with the little girl and was never able to leave the room without a hug from Chrissy and her "I love you" sign. But so far Jenni felt no real direction to join Ballet Shekinah. Perhaps she needed some time. She was confident that God knew exactly what she needed and would supply it at just the right time.

Jenni walked into the music room and was immediately surrounded by children. They were especially excited today because they were having a party.

"Mm-mm, those cookies look good," Jenni said, noticing how the children eyed the treats that Karen was placing on a table.

"Are we going to dance?" she asked the little ones around her.

"Yes!" they all yelled in unison.

"Okay!" Jenni put on some jazz music and stepped away from them. "You're on your own. Let me see you dance."

They turned, twisted, and wiggled. Jenni pretended to play a saxophone and that quickly caught on as one after the other imitated her. She marched around the floor in parade style and everyone followed as if she were a pied piper. The music ended and Karen clapped for them. They all bowed with no prompting. Jenni laughed with delight.

"That was great," Jenni said. "Now what will it be, cookies and surprises," she asked, holding up a sack of gift-wrapped boxes, "or more music?"

The children ran to Jenni, overpowering her so that she sat on the floor surrounded by eager faces as she gave out the gifts she had bought especially for each one.

Karen served cookies and juice. Chrissy came and stood beside Jenni, still holding her gift. She signed the word "dance."

"Okay, Chrissy," Jenni said. "But open your package first."

Chrissy sat on the floor and tore the paper from the box, then dumped its contents in her lap. It was a tiny pink tutu. Jenni helped her put the short ballet skirt on over her shorts.

"Now you can dance."

Chrissy's face lit up with excitement and she ran to the mirror to see herself. Jenni put on some music and Chrissy began to dance, all the while watching Jenni, who stood to the side directing her movements.

The child stretched her small arms above her head and stood on tiptoe. She pranced around the room in a circular motion, then tried to turn in a *pirouette*. The music ended and Chrissy ran into Jenni's arms.

Jenni hugged her tightly. "Chrissy, you were wonderful! Someday I'm going to get you onstage."

Jenni stopped short with the statement. She would never get Chrissy or any of the other children onstage. She wouldn't be here. A sharp sadness came over her, and she decided it was time to leave.

"You'd better go eat your cookies, Chrissy," she said gently.

Chrissy grinned up at her before running to the other children. Jenni walked over to a chair to collect her things. Stephen came over and hugged her.

"This is your last day, too, isn't it, Jenni?"

"Yes, Stephen, it is."

"I'll miss you. I wish you could stay and come back when school starts again. I know Trey wants you to stay, too."

Jenni felt her eyes begin to sting and knew she would cry if she didn't leave soon. She hugged Stephen again. "Good-bye, Stephen. I'll miss you, too."

Karen walked over and hugged her. "I still say you belong here."

Jenni forced a smile. She turned to look at the giggling group of boys and girls. "Would you tell them good-bye for me? I just can't do it."

"What about Trey? Aren't you going to tell him about working with the kids?"

"No. You can tell him if you want, but be sure it's after I leave. Besides, he probably knows already. These kids don't keep secrets well." They both laughed and relieved a little of the tension.

Jenni hugged Karen again. "Be sure to let me know about the baby." She turned quickly to leave and ran into Chrissy, who was standing between Jenni and the door, looking up at her.

"Chrissy, I have to go," Jenni said without bending down for the hug the child usually gave her on leaving the room.

The little girl stared at her with big brown eyes. Not trusting her emotions, Jenni said good-bye and started to walk out the door. Chrissy ran after her, grabbing her around the waist. Jenni knelt down and looked into the little girl's face.

"I love you very much, Chrissy, but I can't stay." It was taking all the strength she had to keep from crying. "Somehow you must know that I won't be back." She smiled and stroked Chrissy's long dark hair. "I know you don't understand why

I'm leaving," she said, her voice quivering. "Sometimes I don't understand either, but I have to go."

Chrissy threw her arms around Jenni, hugging her tight, and the tears she could no longer hold back streamed down Jenni's cheeks. She kissed Chrissy's forehead, then pulled herself away.

"Good-bye, sweetheart," she said and quickly walked out the door.

Once outside the room she leaned her back against the door, closed her eyes, and let hot tears roll down her cheeks. *Why, Lord, why?* she asked silently. *I was just beginning to love them.*

"Jenni!"

Her eyes flew open to see Trey standing before her.

"What's wrong?" He looked at her with a troubled expression.

"Nothing is wrong." She searched through her purse for a tissue, then took the white handkerchief Trey offered. "What are you doing here?" she asked.

"Shouldn't the question be reversed?" He smiled at her and took the handkerchief and dabbed her eyes.

"I've been. . .working with the kids." Trey stood so close she was certain she could feel his breath against her hair. Her heart pounded and her hands felt shaky.

"I know," he said softly. "I need to talk with you, Jenni."

"Don't you think it's a little late for that?" She looked into his clear blue eyes, wishing she didn't love him so much.

"Yes, but hopefully not too late."

"Well, I'm afraid it is." She started to walk away, but Trey took hold of her arm.

"Jenni, please don't leave. At least, not like this."

"What do you care? You're the one that walked out. Remember? So just leave me alone." She tried to pull away, but he took hold of both her arms and faced her squarely.

"I love you, Jenni, and I'm not going to leave you alone."

"I'm not going to listen to this."

"Just give me a chance to—"

"You had your chance!" She was nearly screaming and her words echoed down the hall.

"Come on." He led her into the speech room. "You're going to listen! Then you can walk out if you want."

Jenni walked over to the window, then turned around. "It doesn't matter what you have to say. It can never work."

"I think it can." He walked toward her.

"Well, I don't." She wished he wouldn't come so close or look at her the way he did. Suddenly her emotions broke. "Trey, you wouldn't even let me explain." The tears started again, and she lowered her head so he couldn't see.

He took hold of her chin and tilted her face up toward him. "I know, sweetheart, and I am so sorry. I know that isn't sufficient, but seeing that guy kissing you, and thinking you might care about him. . . . Well, I lost my temper. Again!"

They both smiled at that.

"It wasn't the temper so much as your lack of faith in me."

"I know that, Jenni. And you might not believe this, but once I got past my anger, I never doubted your love for a minute."

Jenni looked at him with surprise. "Then why? All this time. . .is your pride that strong?"

"No. But your faith is and I thought you deserved better than what I could give you. Remember when you told me that you believed God had a special person for your life?"

Jenni nodded her agreement and lowered her head so that she wouldn't have to look into his face. It would have been easier to have just left without seeing him again.

"Well, I thought about that a lot and figured I couldn't possibly be that person. I had hurt you enough and I thought if I stayed out of your life, you might be able to go back to Oklahoma and resume your relationship with Doug. In spite of what I felt, he actually seemed like a nice guy, and you told me he was a Christian. I just thought you deserved that kind of person. I had messed up your life enough."

Jenni wished he would just stop. The pain was too great and the tears wouldn't stop. Trey cupped her face in his hands and wiped the tears from her cheeks with his thumbs. "Sweetheart, I was wrong. I love you more than anything or anyone in this world and I can't let you go." She tried to turn her face away, but Trey turned her back to face him.

"I even talked with Pastor White."

"What?" The shock must have shown on Jenni's face.

He drew her into his arms and hugged her to him. "That's right. And I finally did what I should have done years ago." He pushed her slightly away from him and looked down at her. "I finally got my life straight with God."

"Trey, are you serious?" This was the man she had always suspected was hiding behind the anger and bitterness toward God. "You really gave your life to Christ?" He was smiling down at her. "I don't know what to say."

"Hey, you're the only person that ever confronted me about my anger and bitterness. And you were right. After Katie died I decided I didn't need God. I was even thinking about going into the ministry before that happened." Jenni raised questioning eyes. "Yes, that's why I have a little knowledge of the Bible."

"And now?" She still wasn't sure where this left their relationship.

"Now I know that God used that incident to guide me into the right profession. But most of all, I know that I need Him more than ever because I'm about to ask the most beautiful person in this world to be my wife." He looked at her tenderly. "And I can't be the kind of husband you need without God."

Jenni stared at him in amazement.

"I don't know if I can ever make up for the way I hurt you, but I promise I'll never walk out of your life again. Never!"

Jenni stood silently as Trey continued. "I love you, sweetheart. I want to spend the rest of my life with you. Please tell me you'll marry me."

Before Jenni could say anything, Karen burst into the speech room. "Trey, I'm sorry to disturb you, but I really need your help. I can't get Chrissy calmed down and can't understand what she wants."

Jenni and Trey followed Karen to the music room. Trey knelt down in front of the crying child. "Chrissy, what's wrong? Show me what you want."

Chrissy looked beyond Trey, her breath coming in sobbing gulps. "J–Jenni!"

Jenni froze in her steps, not believing what she heard.

"Jenni!" Chrissy called again, arms raised.

Jenni scooped the child up in her arms and danced around in circles. "Chrissy, you said my name! You said my name!" She hugged the child to her. "Oh, sweetheart, I can't believe it. You said my name."

Chrissy kept her arms locked around Jenni's neck as they twirled round and round. Finally Jenni stopped and turned to Trey. "She said my name. Did you hear her? She said 'Jenni.' "

Trey circled his arms around both of them. "Yes, and I'm still waiting to hear what you say. Will you marry me?"

"Yes! Yes!"

epilogue

Jenni was frantically checking each child's costume when Trey appeared backstage. "What are you doing here? You're supposed to be out front taking pictures."

"Don't worry, I won't miss a single picture of your young protégés."

Stephen came up behind her. "Ho, ho, ho."

"Oh, Stephen, you make a wonderful Santa," she said, patting his padded stomach.

As she straightened the ribbon in Chrissy's hair, Trey raised the camera and snapped a quick picture. "Trey!"

He put his hands up in defense. "I'm going. I'm going." The children giggled and Jenni helped them find their places onstage before the curtain went up.

Lyn came over to the group. "Okay, guys and gals, are you ready?" They all nodded their agreement. "Good. Your audience is waiting." She turned aside to Jenni. "By the way," she whispered, "is the teacher still holding up?"

"Just barely!" Jenni gave an exasperated look. "Shouldn't you be out front to introduce the performance?"

Lyn smiled. "Ordinarily, I introduce any program held at Ballet Shekinah, especially when one of my lead dancers is involved." She gave Jenni a hug. "But someone asked a special favor of me."

Jenni looked puzzled, then heard Trey's voice on the microphone.

"Ladies and gentlemen," his clear voice resonated through the sound system. "May I present the dance class of my wife, Mrs. Jenni Lawson Maddox."

Jenni smiled at Trey's introduction. God had certainly been working His share of miracles in her life these last months.

First the job with Ballet Shekinah, then the wedding, and now the Christmas performance.

She quickly turned her attention back to the children. "Okay, kids. You'll do great." She rushed offstage just as the curtain came up.

"Ho, ho, ho," Stephen laughed as he filled stockings on a cardboard fireplace. Then he yawned and sat down in a chair beside the Christmas tree, pretending to fall asleep.

The children were sitting around the tree, dressed as toys and packages. The music started and she motioned them forward. Nobody moved. Jenni felt a little panic rise in her. How many times had she brought them to this stage so it wouldn't seem foreign to them? Finally they stood up and lined up onstage. They kicked, turned, and waddled like ducks, awkward in their costumes. Jenni couldn't help but think what a cute chorus line they made—little synchronized Christmas toys and packages. At that moment Patrick started in the other direction. *Well, maybe not exactly synchronized,* she admitted. The children bowed when the music ended and the audience clapped.

The program continued as each child did a special routine. There was a wooden soldier, a jack-in-the-box, gift-wrapped packages, and, of course, a ballerina. Chrissy waved at Trey when he took her picture, then put her arms out to her sides and circled the stage, her long hair flying. Then after a *demi plié*, she ended her performance with a *pirouette*. Jenni glanced at the audience from the side stage. She could see smiles, whispers, and positive nods of the head. The children were making a great impression.

After a few more numbers they all walked together onstage and bowed to the audience. Stephen came over and pulled Jenni onstage.

"Thank you so much for coming," Jenni said. "The children have worked very hard and I can't tell you how proud I am of them." She looked at the little performers at her side. "We have one more number and that will close our program."

Backstage Jenni and Lyn quickly changed the children's costumes to long white robes with gold tinsel circling their waists, while Trey and some of the performers from Ballet Shekinah replaced the Christmas tree with a nativity scene. Karen, her husband, and new baby boy depicted Mary, Joseph, and the Christ child. Each child carried a plastic cylinder that held a lighted flashlight, giving the illusion of candlelight. They marched onstage to the strains of "Silent Night." The five little angels circled baby Jesus. Stephen, now dressed in a suit and tie, stepped to the microphone. "Would you sing with us?"

The audience joined with the children's voices. "Silent night! holy night! . . ." Trey walked over, put his arm around Jenni, and sang out in his baritone voice.

When the song ended, Chrissy stepped to the microphone. She signed a message, then said aloud, "Merry Christmas and God bless you."

Jenni looked up at her smiling husband. "God has already blessed us," she said quietly, and offered a silent prayer of thanksgiving.

A Letter To Our Readers

Dear Reader:

In order that we might better contribute to your reading enjoyment, we would appreciate your taking a few minutes to respond to the following questions. We welcome your comments and read each form and letter we receive. When completed, please return to the following:

Rebecca Germany, Fiction Editor
Heartsong Presents
PO Box 719
Uhrichsville, Ohio 44683

1. Did you enjoy reading *Dance from the Heart?*
   ❑ Very much. I would like to see more books by this author!
   ❑ Moderately
   I would have enjoyed it more if ________________

   ____

   ____

2. Are you a member of **Heartsong Presents**? Yes ❑ No ❑
   If no, where did you purchase this book?______________

   ____

3. How would you rate, on a scale from 1 (poor) to 5 (superior), the cover design?______________________

4. On a scale from 1 (poor) to 10 (superior), please rate the following elements.

   _____ Heroine   _____ Plot

   _____ Hero   _____ Inspirational theme

   _____ Setting   _____ Secondary characters

5. These characters were special because________________

____

____

6. How has this book inspired your life?________________

____

____

7. What settings would you like to see covered in future **Heartsong Presents** books?________________________

____

____

8. What are some inspirational themes you would like to see treated in future books?__________________________

____

____

9. Would you be interested in reading other **Heartsong Presents** titles? Yes ❑ No ❑

10. Please check your age range:
❑ Under 18 ❑ 18-24 ❑ 25-34
❑ 35-45 ❑ 46-55 ❑ Over 55

11. How many hours per week do you read?______________

Name ____

Occupation _______________________________________

Address ____

City __________________ State ____________ Zip __________